Be Near Me

Ian McDiarmid is an actor. He was Joint Artistic Director of the Almeida Theatre, London, from 1990 to 2001. His extensive career includes leading roles with all the major British companies. He won a Tony Award for his performance in Brian Friel's *Faith Healer* on Broadway. Recently, he appeared in *John Gabriel Borkman* at the Donmar Warehouse and *Six Characters in Search of an Author* in the West End. His adaptation of *Be Near Me* is his first play.

Andrew O'Hagan was born in Glasgow in 1968. He has written three novels. He previously won the James Tait Black Memorial Prize for Fiction, was twice nominated for the Booker Prize, and won the E. M. Forster Award from the American Academy of Arts and Letters. He lives in London.

IAN McDIARMID

Be Near Me

adapted from the novel by

ANDREW O'HAGAN

faber and faber

First published in Great Britain in 2009
by Faber and Faber Limited
74–77 Great Russell Street, London WC1B 3DA

Typeset by Country Setting, Kingsdown, Kent CT14 8ES
Printed in England by CPI Bookmarque, Croydon, Surrey

A CIP record for this book
is available from the British Library

ISBN 978-0-571-24968-8

2 4 6 8 10 9 7 5 3 1

To Alex Miklaszewicz

Introduction

ANDREW O'HAGAN

When I was very young, I thought the theatre was a place where higher beings went about their celestial business, as if they knew nothing of ordinary life and its political mysteries. I went to the Gaiety Theatre in Ayr and saw a troop of beautiful dancers up on their toes, making a jealous suitor dance himself to death. I went to the Palace Theatre in Kilmarnock and watched an opera based on *Hansel and Gretel*, where, for mysterious reasons, the children of a poor woodcutter are sent into the forest. They try to survive by eating a house made of sweets, before returning home and putting a bad old woman in the oven. It didn't seem to me at the time that these dramatic stories had anything to do with my life: they were enchantments, stories promoting a strictly magical notion of life, where even threatened people lived happily ever after. It would take years for me to understand what the fears lurking in those cardboard forests of Ayrshire actually represented – abandonment, hunger, sexual obsession, imprisonment – but I've never forgotten that first period when all theatre appeared to me like a form of surreal niceness.

Things changed one day when a nice caretaker allowed me to look inside the long defunct Britannia Panopticon Music Hall in Glasgow's Trongate: it was an eerie place where one imagined laughter and the remnants of Edwardian applause still clinging to the wallpaper, and to this day the place appears to me in dreams. I knew that Stan Laurel had performed at the Britannia in the days before he moved to Hollywood, and that Harry Lauder and Dan Leno had given Glasgow audiences a horde of comedy culled from everyday experience and patter. When I began learning about the kinds of shows and the kinds of audience that came to the Britannia, I understood that something strangely democratic had occurred there, and that large investments of common feeling must constitute a sort of political power. Later still, in an archive I came across a letter that was found on the floor of a burning Glasgow theatre. It said simply, 'It won't happen unless we make it happen.' Nobody knows who wrote the letter or for whose eyes it was meant, but in my mind it conjures an idea of the theatre as a site of assignations, romantic and otherwise, that might threaten to change a person's life.

If you come from a world of aspiration, as Glasgow was, with its beautiful public parks and its once gleaming high-rises, then the theatre could easily come to seem like a place where the idea of human improvement was essential. In the 1970s, that idea seemed to take on a perfect form when the company 7:84, under John McGrath, began presenting plays that married the energy of Variety to a dormant political radicalism. There was no National Theatre of Scotland in those days, but 7:84, along with the productions of Wildcat, Clyde Unity Theatre, and Borderline (then based in my native Irvine New Town), appeared to take on our national mythologies and social turmoil in a way that was attached to the everyday political nature of the people. And I don't just mean theatre people, but the kind of people who didn't consider themselves to be part of the usual audience for serious plays. It might be that those early political productions added to my sense of what was possible for a novelist when I turned out to be one: there was lyrical realism at work in those productions, and I thought of them as providing a new spectacle and a new philosophy based on lived experience, much as American plays of the 1930s to the mid-50s had done. I see when I look back that the first proper thing I ever wrote was a Tennessee Williams kind of story called *Orpheus Ascending*, about an old woman in Glasgow's

Royal Infirmary who wished someone would come and do her make-up.

That felt like a kind of politics and a kind of dreaming. It also felt like a species of memory and I'm sure was the sort of writing pressed into being by notions of a changing society. Thatcher was more than just a little bit around by then, and the theatre, with varying degrees of success, continued to seem like a place where people might go to meet their morality. It also seemed like a firm platform for dissent. I remember a number of productions at Glasgow's Citizens' Theatre around that time, the late 1980s, that were so sumptuous and so clever that I'm sure the audience scanned every expression for news and for evidence about the political times we happened to be living through. Perhaps the most memorable was Philip Prowse's production of *The Vortex*, starring Rupert Everett and Maria Aitken, in which one generation turns on the other: the younger one is shocked by the older one's faithlessness, whilst the mother is shocked by the extent of her son's hedonism. This was around the time the Berlin Wall collapsed, the time when students were murdered in Tiananmen Square, when the Ayatollah condemned Salman Rushdie. And there we were, watching *The Vortex*, and I strongly believe the production made a beeline for the audience's common uncertainty: the night I saw it, more than half the people in the audience were sitting in subsidised seats (UB40-holders went free and students paid £1) and it is not easy to describe the level of engagement the play provoked. Afterwards, people were loudly discussing the play as they walked through the Gorbals and some of us sat in city-centre bars arguing the toss about everything. It seemed that plays, even what some considered a languid old play about toffs, could, if beautifully made and performed, stir people to battle with their own ideas and circumstances in a spirit of changefulness.

There was another play like that, which I first saw in London and which I later travelled to Dublin to see in a separate production. That play was *Faith Healer* by Brian Friel, and each version starred Ian McDiarmid as the strangely captivating, deluded impresario Teddy. The play stirred what to me were chiefly political emotions, to do with the power of belief and the meaning of the past. Suddenly, so much of what I'd considered to matter about the theatre, from the faraway days of those Ayrshire enchantments to the social aliveness of those plays produced by 7:84 and at the Citz, came together in a single production and I wanted to believe much more of it was possible.

Out of the blue, then, in 2007, came a message from the director John Tiffany that an adaptation of my novel *Be Near Me* was proposed by none other than Ian McDiarmid. I read Ian's adaptation immediately and felt he might have made the story new for the stage. I thought it was full of sensitive possibilities: Ian seemed to see Father David, the central character, as in many ways an actor, performing a life rather than living one. The central character was also a man in exile from the truth of himself and the pressure of the past. Mrs Poole, the housekeeper, was always to me the moral conscience of the story, and the play made it seem possible that she could become a figure of commanding power. It all remains to be seen. The theatre, at least to me, so often embodies hope and hard work, and I read the adaptation believing that the voices of the characters were bidding for a political conversation of the most tender and unusual kind. I hoped that the stage version of *Be Near Me*, co-produced with the Donmar Warehouse, would engage people at the levels of laughter and passion and moral rumination, everything I had had in mind when I first conceived the characters and worked to bring them to the kind of reality that matters in a literary work. The story is a hymn to not being alone – to that Tennysonian nearness that gave the novel its title.

I have used the words hope and possibility, and that is as far as an author should go in contemplating what seems a fine opportunity for something of one's own to have a new and separate life. It will be for others to take hold of the piece and identify its qualities. I see in the end that enchantment and the political dimension may have come together for me when I wrote *Be Near Me*, and they may do so again, in another way, in the play that is set to emerge from the imaginations of Ian McDiarmid and John Tiffany. The characters in *Be Near Me* come from a genuine place, a Britain that is more than one country and more than one ideal, but it always seemed exciting to me that these people might eventually have the chance to find a home in the pure imaginative space of the theatre, where human figures may be seen to come alive as they turn in the light and speak to the dark.

Be Near Me received its first performance at the Palace Theatre, Kilmarnock, on 16 January 2009, before transferring to the Donmar Warehouse, London, on 22 January 2009. The cast, in alphabetical order, was as follows:

Mr Nolan/Mr McCallum/Mr Hamilton
  Jimmy Chisholm
Mrs Poole Blythe Duff
Mrs Nolan/Angela/Mrs Fraser Kathryn Howden
Father David Anderton Ian McDiarmid
Cameron/Father Damian David McGranaghan
Mark Richard Madden
Lisa Helen Mallon
Mrs Anderton Colette O'Neil
Mr Poole/Voice of the Sheriff Benny Young
Mr Dorran/Bishop Gerard Jimmy Yuill

Director John Tiffany
Designer Peter McKintosh
Lighting Designer Guy Hoare
Sound Designer Gareth Fry
Musical Director Davey Anderson
Associate Sound Designer Matthew Padden
Assistant Director Abbey Wright

Characters

in order of appearance

Father David Anderton

Mrs Poole

Mr Dorran

Lisa

Cameron

Mark

Mrs Nolan

Mr Nolan

Mr Poole

Mrs Anderton

Bishop Gerard

Father Damian

Angela

Mr McCallum

Policeman

Mrs Fraser

Mr Hamilton

Voice of the Clerk

Voice of the Sheriff

BE NEAR ME

Act One

A church bell. Darkness. A voice.

Father David
'Be near me when my light is low,
When the blood creeps, and the nerves prick
And tingle; and the heart is sick,
And all the wheels of Being slow.'

Light slowly reaches Father David Anderton.

'Be near me when the sensuous frame
Is rack'd with pangs that conquer trust;
And Time, a maniac scattering dust,
And Life, a Fury slinging flame.'

Other voices now. A sectarian song.

'Be near me when my faith is dry,
And men the flies of latter spring,
That lay their eggs, and sting and sing
And weave their petty cells and die.'

The song takes over from the poem.
Men and women of West Ayrshire. Silhouettes
against a grey sky.
Father David jangles his keys. A Chopin Nocturne
takes over from the song.
A dusty chandelier. A faded Persian rug. Two chairs.
A table set for one.

SCENE ONE

Mrs Poole '*Potage du père tranquille*'.

Mrs Poole has stepped from the men and women and, with a flourish, indicates lunch.

The best abstinence money can buy.

Father David Goodness. Lettuce soup.

Father David puts his keys on the table and sits.

Do you think we could go wild and add the odd dod of *pain de campagne*?

Mrs Poole Well, if you want to remember Christ's agony by gorging on crusts, I can't stop you. You'll recall there's a dirty great sponge of vinegar being presented to his face as we speak.

Father David And there's some of last night's Alsace in the fridge.

Mrs Poole Bloody hell. When I was a girl, Good Friday was a day for closing the curtains and hanging your head.

She leaves for the kitchen.

Father David Even at this sad time, we must have gaiety.
  After two services, and an hour's teaching in prospect, I'm looking for laughter today.

Father David notices some specks of dust on the table. He looks up.
  Light has faded on the men and women. The Chopin track has completed.

Did I tell you this chandelier was hung in my first set of rooms in Balliol?
  I used to stare up at it instead of writing essays on the English Civil War. Can you imagine?

A present from one of the Anderton aunts. She thought it criminal for a young man to have to study under an oil lamp. It was almost as dust-laden then.

He polishes his spoon with his napkin.
Mrs Poole returns with the bread and the wine.

Mrs Poole Don't get me started, Father David. There's enough work to be done here without me bothering about your daft lights. While you were gazing at the ceiling among your dreaming spires, my sister and I were working the night shift up here in Dalgarnock.

Father David All that stuff. It seems so mysterious to me now.

Mrs Poole bends to smooth the rug.

Mrs Poole Well, you've a bit of an education up your sleeve, Father, and you're just like me, you like your things around you.

She straightens up with some difficulty, and pours the wine, taking a very little for herself.

People here go on like their home is a prison.

Father David Do they? I'm sure your husband doesn't for one.

Mrs Poole Oh, Jack just cuts grass and drinks his whisky.

She sits.

When I walked in here a couple of weeks ago, I saw straight away it's a place for thinking.

Father David I don't know about that, Mrs Poole.

Mrs Poole Anyway, I've finally found my job, and a person who knows how to put a sentence together.

She holds her glass up to the light before taking a sip.

Father David Don't be too hard on Dalgarnock, or your husband. People here are no different from anywhere else, except they probably have more to deal with and smaller means to do it.

Mrs Poole You'll find out if I'm too hard on them.

A slight pause.

Jack doesn't know me. You know me better than him.

Father David I only know a few old prayers and a dozen facts about Proust.

Mrs Poole That's a damn sight more than this lot. Most of them around here wouldn't give you daylight in a dark corner.

Father David Is that a Scottish expression?

Mrs Poole Your mother would know it. (*She sighs.*) They wouldn't give you the shine off their sweat.

Father David (*laughing*) Proust would be proud of you. So would my mother.

Mrs Poole You know what I mean. You can't expect a priest to know much about life, but at least you've read a couple of books.

Another pause.

Don't let it get cold.

Father David Whatever you say. How's the wine?

Mrs Poole *Parfait.*

Father David You have a nice tone to your pronunciation, Mrs Poole.

Mrs Poole Thank you.

She pours herself a little more.

St Andrew's evening classes are not exactly Balliol College.

Father David And none the worse, I'm sure, for that.

She goes to fill his glass.

Steady on. I've got fourth-year 'special needs' for World Religion in half an hour.

Mrs Poole Then I imagine you'll need this.

Father David They are a tonic in themselves.

A slight pause.

Mrs Poole Has France always been your favourite? I mean of all the places you've been.

Father David Well, it's created some personable Englishmen.

Mrs Poole What do you mean?

Father David A little contact with France does an Englishman no end of good. But too much of it can make the French intolerable.

Mrs Poole Is that a joke?

Father David Depends if you're English or French.

Mrs Poole And what if you're Scots?

Father David Bad luck.

Mrs Poole God, you're a pain. One minute you're Scottish yourself and the next minute you're more English than Churchill.

Father David Comes of having a father from Lancashire and an Edinburgh mum.

Mrs Poole I don't think you see enough of her.

Father David She hates being disturbed when she's writing.
She's in Paris, as it happens, researching her latest.

Mrs Poole She's a busy woman.

Father David She'll be flying back via Glasgow, so we might see her next week.

Mrs Poole I would like to go to France some day. See the vineyards.

Father David (*draining his glass*) Alsace is in the north-east.

Mrs Poole Like Aberdeen.

Father David *Exactement.*

They exchange smiles. Father David picks up his keys.
The men and women silhouetted once more, singing something undistinguished from the Catholic hymn book.

As the hymn ends, the men and women leave, revealing the backs of the pupils of the fourth-year 'special needs' class at St Andrew's Academy. An animal presence against a brilliant orange sky.

The chapel house and Mrs Poole disappear.

Mr Dorran, Head of Music, comes down with an armful of violins.

SCENE TWO

Father David Mr Dorran, I made a request of you just after Lent.

Let us not have any more of those rubbishy hymns, with their horrible words about sunny days and being happy.

Mr Dorran Father Anderton, those hymns have been used in Scottish schools for quite some time. They are very popular. The pupils like to sing them.

8

Father David They also like to sing Puff Daddy, Mr Dorran, and we shan't be introducing him into the Mass just yet.

Mr Dorran If you'll excuse me, I'm awful busy. This was supposed to be a day off.

Father David Could you not have managed 'Cross of Jesus' since it's Easter?

Mr Dorran I don't know it.

Father David Music by John Stainer. Words by William Sparrow-Simpson.

Mr Dorran Why do you patronise me in this way every time I see you?

Father David Mr Dorran, I'm not asking for the 'Stabat Mater'.

Mr Dorran Yes, you are. In the context, yes, you are.

He plucks a string.

Has it ever occurred to you that you don't belong here, Father David? This is a Scottish comprehensive, not Eton College.

Father David Heaven forfend.

Mr Dorran You know what this town is? It's an unemployment black spot. I don't think you understand what has happened here. The factories are empty. The churches are empty –

Father David – but the heart is full.

Mr Dorran You should take a leaf out of Bishop Gerard's book. He comes here with the crook and everything else, but he'll also sit down at the piano and play Boyzone to get the pupils' attention.

Father David Ah, but then Gerard has a much wider range than I do.

Mr Dorran leaves. Father David moves to face his class, who are now occupying three of several chairs. Still only their backs.

Lisa Mad. Totally mad. We had to wear shit scarves and everythin'.

Cameron And nae shoes. And yer no' allowed to mix. Girls went in one place, us intae another.

Father David But what did your visit teach you?

Lisa They chop off women's hands for nothin'.

Mark They eat bull's cocks.

Lisa laughs. We see Mark's face for the first time.

It's all suicide bombers and everythin'. One minute you're jeest walking down the street, and then the next people are getting blown up and dying everywhere. Totally nuts.

More laughter.
A sudden America-themed explosion of energy from Mark and Lisa.
An animalistic collage: terrorist 're-enactments'; hip-hop etc. Chairs are overturned.
Father David watches.
Cameron, who has a cold, reluctantly joins in.

Cameron You're jeest prejudiced, McNulty.

Mark Shut it, Ca-Ca.

Cameron The name's Cameron.

Mark Shut it, Cameraman.

Father David All right, now. Come on. What else did you learn at the mosque?

Lisa It was real creepy.

Father David That's not very thoughtful.

Lisa It's true but.

Mark Check this out. It stank. They're all bloody thingmies. Bloody asylum-seekers.

Cameron You shouldn't let him say that, Father. You talk shite, McNulty.

Mark Fuck off, Cameraman.

Father David Language.

Mark Whatever.
  Don't ask us if you don't want to learn. It was a total dump.
  Disagree with them and they throw acid in your face.

Cameron Evidence! Show us yer evidence, McNulty.

Lisa Aw, shut it, Cammy. He puts on this big act. He's always droppin' science about shit he knows nothin' about.

Mark Stop Xeroxing me, bitch. I'll walk Cameraman down by myself, no problem. All this shit about camel-jockeys.

Father David Please. I won't have names in here.

  Mark winks at Lisa.

Mark All right, Father. But you've got to admit terrorists are terrorists.

Cameron They're not terrorists. They just believe in their own religion.

Mark Who's asking you, dweeb?

Cameron Catholics put bombs in chip shops in Northern Ireland.

Mark Get a grip. It's no' people from this country that drive planes into people's offices and make bombs out of banana smoothies. We don't take folk hostage and machete their heads off.

Why don't you get your wee boyfriend on the back of yer fairy cycle and go and live in fucken Gayland or wherever it is you get your ideas from.

Father David Now, that's quite enough. We won't have that kind of language in here. Understand?

Mark Whit language? The Scottish language?

Father David No, that's fine. Let's just do without the expletives.

Mark That is our language, Father.

He starts to sing some sectarian and obscene words to a Celtic football song. Lisa sniggers and joins in, hip-hop fashion.

Cameron tidies the chairs and then leaves.

Mark softly croons a verse in the direction of Father David.

Father David So that's your tribe. A football club.

Mark Celtic's no' a tribe. It's a tradition. You've got tae have your team.

Lisa He thinks Celtic's gonna win the European Cup.

Mark The UEFA Cup.

Lisa That's why he's so happy.

Mark This could be the best year we've ever had. Did you see that Liverpool game at Anfield? That was bitchin'. Totally awesome. To beat Liverpool on their own soil!

Father David I used to like Liverpool.

Lisa Traitor!

Father David Not the team. I don't know anything about football. The place. The people.

Mark Best night I've had so far.

Lisa Yeh. Aiden McGeady.

Father David Is he Irish?

Lisa Born in Glasgow.

Mark Pure magic. Even I would shag him.

Father David Language.

> *The Celtic song again. More voices. Men and women silhouetted. Mark, Lisa and Father David are now outside.*
> *The sky is a deep evening blue.*

Mark Father, in your whole life have you ever had sex?

Lisa You've got to answer.

Father David No, I don't.

Mark Come on. Get over yourself.

Father David Get over myself? Is that another one of your American television phrases?

Mark Whatever. Come on, Father. Yes or no.

Father David I've no intention of answering a question like that.

Lisa He has! That's awesome, man.

Mark I know he has. Or he'd have just said 'No'.

Father David Don't be so idiotic.

Mark Don't sweat it, Father. We're all human.

Father David I have my doubts about that.

Mark Yeh. Like Arabs.

Light has faded on the men and women.

Father David Did you really have such a bad time at the mosque?

Mark Damn right. These people just want to hurt people.

Lisa They're mad as shit. Sorry, Father. They hate our way of life.

Mark You got that from the telly, bitch.

Lisa Bite me.

He does. She screams and tries to bite him back.
An animal dance.
Father David stares at them.
The sound of the waves.

Father David America is out there somewhere. Beyond that rock. Have you been there?

Mark America?

Lisa Get real.

Father David Ailsa Craig.

Mark Paddy's Milestone? Just an old rock covered in bird shit. Why would anybody go there?

Father David Because it's beautiful, Mark.

Lisa It's always been there.

Father David Exactly. You've both lived here all your lives, haven't you? What, fifteen years? And Ailsa Craig has been out there every day. Don't you wonder what it's like?

Lisa I know what it's like. It's boring.

Father David No, you're boring. There are no people out there.
  Just a world on its own in the middle of the sea.

Mark No government.

Lisa No nothing.
  Come on. I'm starvin'.

Father David It's a bird sanctuary.

Lisa See you at the wedding.

Father David Wedding?

Mark You're marrying her sister.

Father David Oh. Am I?

Mark Part of your job description, Father.

Father David Call me David.

Mark Call me Cardinal.

The sound of the waves.

Lisa Come on, McNuggets!

Mark and Lisa leave.
  Father David takes out his keys.
  He finds himself recalling some lines of Shakespeare.

Father David
  'Blame not this haste of mine. If you mean well,
  Now go with me and with this holy man
  Into the chantry by: there before him,
  And underneath that consecrated roof,
  Plight me the full assurance of your faith;
  That my most jealous and too doubtful soul
  May live at peace.'

'Three Times a Lady'.
  The wedding disco.
  Red balloons. Tartan.
  The men and women career through; drunken
dancing; arguments about the catering; someone being
sick etc.
  Mrs Nolan, the mother of the bride, comes forward.

SCENE THREE

Mrs Nolan Just beautiful, Father. You gave oor Helen a great send-off. We've set you a wee place at oor table.

Father David That's very kind of you, Mrs Nolan, but I really mustn't stay. I've a great deal of parish business to get on with.

Mr Nolan approaches.

Mr Nolan Are we no' good enough for you then, Father Anderton?

Mrs Nolan Stay and have a wee dram. Just for me. It's no' every day a person sees their oldest lassie getting married.

Lisa and Mark are at the other side of the room. A nod to Father David implies 'Do as you're told'.

Father David All right. That would be splendid.

He puts his keys away. Mrs Nolan drifts back to her guests.

Mr Nolan Would you look at the state ae them? Uncaged beasts. You'd think they never had a day oot in their lives.

Father David You were born in Dalgarnock, Mr Nolan?

Mr Nolan Born and bred. And I'll tell you something for nothing. It's no longer the place I grew up in.

Father David How so?

Mr Nolan I'll tell you how. There used to be plenty of work about here. Good jobs. Coal mining for one and a big steel works over the river. That ICI place used to employ thousands making paint, and before that it was Nobel making explosives. Men worked in those places for forty years and, at the end of it, the Jobcentre was trying to turn them into Avon ladies.

Father David Is that right?

Mr Nolan You're damn right it's right. That's your global economy for you. Experienced tradesmen working in pet shops. And that's the lucky ones.

He looks over at Mark and Lisa.

And these younger ones leaving school? Well, they wouldn't want jobs even if there were jobs to give them.

Mrs Nolan has returned with a drink for Father David.

Mrs Nolan You'd put years on a person the way you talk. Put a smile on your face, for heaven's sake.

Mr Nolan He's as well to know the truth. This used to be a good place to rear children. Now it's just an open-air asylum. Indian restaurants and Christ knows what else, and no jobs for the locals.
    But I don't suppose you know very much about the working classes, do you, Father?

Father David I'm a product of the 1960s, Mr Nolan. We assumed we knew everything about the working classes.

Mr Nolan Aye. But you don't know much about your authentic Scottish prol-et-ar-iat, do you?

Father David Well, my life hasn't perhaps been as sheltered as you might think.

Mr Nolan Oh, 'perhaps'. 'Perhaps', is it? 'Perhaps' his life hasn't been as sheltered as we think, Denise.

Mrs Nolan drags her husband back to the dance.

Hey, Mr Perhaps's life is not as sheltered as we think!

Mark comes over.

Mark Not dancing, Father?

Father David I should be going.

Mark But the party's great, man. Totally mad.

Father David Is that good?

Mark Check out these balloons.

He shows Father David some red packets of condoms. Lisa approaches from behind and leans on both their shoulders.

Lisa McNuggets, stop ribbing him.

Mark Multi-ribbed! That's what they are! It says it on here.

Lisa Are you having a nice time, Father? That was a cool speech you made.
My sister's a bitch, actually. But now I have a room to myself. That's all I care about, so it is.

Mark Excuse me, Lisa. If you don't mind, I've just been showing Father Anderton these rubber johnnies.

Father David Yes, and I'm deeply shocked.

Lisa takes one from Mark and places it in Father David's hand.

Lisa And now he's holding one!

I've got the key to their honeymoon suite. We're going to put hordes of johnnies all over their bedroom.

Mark Hey, motherfucker, stop telling everybody.

Lisa Do you think that's a good idea, Father?

Father David Very good. Just don't tell the Bishop.

Mark Or the Pope.

Whoops from the dance floor.

Check them out. Totally fucked up.

Lisa goes back to join them.

Don't go yet. See you out the front in ten.

Mark follows Lisa.
  Father David quickly pockets the condom.
  Mr Nolan returns with a refill and another guest,
Jack Poole, Mrs Poole's husband, who is drunk.

Mr Nolan I love a drink.

Mr Poole It's a Scottish tradition. Good speech, Father.

Father David Thank you, Mr Poole.

Mr Poole Jack.

Mr Nolan I like a drink more than I like any of my children.

Father David Mrs Poole not celebrating today?

Mr Poole She's a bit off colour, Father.

Father David I'm sorry to hear that.

Mr Poole I suppose you spend a lot of your time feeling sorry for people, Father David.

Mr Nolan Whereas me, see, I don't like people very much.

Mr Poole Part of his charm, Father.

Mr Nolan Part of oor national charm. Is that not right, Jack? You must have discovered that by now, Father?

Father David Whatever you say, Mr Nolan. It's your day.

Mr Nolan That's right.

Father David It's your daughter's day.

Mr Nolan You'd better believe it.

He drains his glass.

Our Lisa says you help her and her pals. Up at the school. She says you go places and that.

Mr Poole Good for you.

Mr Nolan But jest watch that lot. Oor Lisa could run rings round a matador.

Father David She's very sweet.

Mr Poole She is that.

Mr Nolan Perhaps.

He offers to fill Father David's glass. He refuses.
A wild and raucous Scottish country dance is now in full swing. Mr Nolan swings towards it.
Mr Poole hesitates for a moment as if about to say something.

Father David Not tripping the light fantastic, Mr Poole?

Mr Poole Two left feet, Father.

Father David Those we have in common.

A slight pause.

Mr Poole It's the Slosh.

Father David I'm sorry?

Mr Poole The Slosh.

Father David The Slosh?

Mr Poole (*indicating inside*) That's the Slosh.

Father David Oh. Is it a Scottish country dance?

Mr Poole It's a dance women do at weddings.

Father David Women only?

Mr Poole It's a West Coast thing.

Father David Do they have one just for men?

A silence.

Mr Poole It's imported from America.

Father David Ah.

Mr Poole Along with their missiles and their air bases.

Father David Part of the package?

Mr Poole But Dominic Nolan says it's a Scottish working-class thing.

Father David Ah, yes. Well, that's his area of expertise.

A slight pause.

Look, please give Mrs Poole my best and tell her I'll manage without her this week, if she's unwell.

Mr Poole She says you're a tonic, Father.

Another pause.

Father David Well, tell her to look after herself. You should too.

Mr Poole stares at Father David.

Look after yourself, I mean.

Mr Poole returns to the bar.
   Father David has joined Mark outside the hotel.
   The sky is a deep blue once more.
   Mark flicks his lighter.

Mark It's cleared up out here.

Father David Yes. Thank goodness.

Mark Escaped her da's evil clutches?

Father David Mr Nolan's all right. He just tends to buttonhole.

Mark He's in a bad mood because he has to pay for all this shit.

Father David While the groom's father gets off scot-free.

Mark Nae justice.
   Mr Fuckface's just puked down the side of his crappy Volvo.

Father David Mr?

Mark Headmaster to you. Piss Head.

Father David You should show some pity, Mark. Mr McCallum's a decent man. He was kind enough to ask me to talk to the seniors about the history of art, and about world religions to you.

Mark So he introduced us like.

Father David In a manner of speaking.

   Mark flicks his lighter.

Mark My da's the fattest man in Ayrshire.

   He flicks again.

He's a fucken joke.

Father David Perhaps he's depressed.

Mark I don't think he likes me.

Father David Nonsense, Mark. Of course your father likes you.

Mark It's nothing to me.

A slight pause.

We went swimming once. He's so fat he made waves that rolled right across the pool. They all shouted at him. I stood shivering at the lockers for ages. It was horrible. I wanted to go back and get him.

Father David Why didn't you?

Mark They were all laughing at him.
   He used to be quite a sharp guy. He had all the cool gear before anybody else.
   He got a trial to play football for Kilmarnock, one time. He used to read books and that.

It's darker now. Stars.

Father David I'll take you and Lisa over to see Ailsa Craig, if you want to.

Mark To the rock? Is there a boat?

Father David I'm sure I could use my influence. If you want to.

Mark I wouldn't mind seeing it. Just the once.

Father David Then leave it to me.

Mark You're mad.

He flicks again.

Father David Maybe you should become a fireman.

Mark No way. It's my job to keep them in work.

Another flick.

Some people would think it weird, wouldn't they, a priest and a young guy gabbin' under the stars?

Father David I'm sure they would.

Mark Well, that's their problem, isn't it? I'm going back to the wedding.

Father David The bright one over there. That's the North Star.

Mark Cool. I wonder if you can, like, see that from America.

Mark returns to the throbbing disco.
A frenzy of bodies in silhouette.

Father David pulls out his keys.
The red condom drops from his pocket.
He picks it up and examines it for a few moments before discarding it.

Another Chopin Nocturne as the chandelier descends.
Mrs Poole is standing at the table, trimming red roses.
On one of the chairs there is a smart coat with a smart piece of hand-luggage beside it. There is a rucksack on the other.

SCENE FOUR

Mrs Poole I wish you'd turn that off. God, I hate watery music.

Father David Poor washerwoman that you are, the famous Scottish education system has barely left its mark on you.

Mrs Poole Chopin. It makes such a fuss of itself. I can't believe your mother likes it.

Father David My mother's musical taste, like much of her life, is in a constant state of flux.

I think at the moment she's going through her Modernist phase. I can't imagine what it's doing to her writing.

Mrs Anderton Not true!

Mrs Anderton comes in with a tissue, bright red from blotting her lipstick. Chopin stops.

Honestly, David, you make it sound like the menopause – which, incidentally, I got two novels out of and sailed through with colours flying.

She is looking for somewhere to put the tissue.
Mrs Poole offers the waste bucket for the cut stalks.
Mrs Anderton lobs it in.

Thank you, Mrs Poole. (*To Father David, as she returns her make-up kit to a side pocket of her luggage.*) That bathroom could do with a bit of touching up. And James MacMillan is not a modernist. He's good Ayrshire stock. Like Rabbie Burns. Not a romantic, perhaps, but he composes from the soul. And – I would venture – that of Scotland.

Mrs Poole (*with a smile*) Scottish soul music.

Mrs Anderton Exactly, Mrs Poole.

Father David From the soul?

Mrs Anderton Well, he's one of your lot, isn't he?

Father David My mother means he's Roman Catholic.

Mrs Anderton I don't think Mrs Poole requires simultaneous translation.

I'm an atheist, Mrs Poole. I would say 'and proud of it' but it's pointless being proud of a fact. I used to claim to be an agnostic, but now I think that's cheating. These days, it's important to show whose side you're on.

Father David You've got to have your team . . . like football.

Mrs Anderton Or politics.

My Jesuitical son is trying to trick me into admitting there's such a thing as 'the soul'. He smiles because he thinks I'm trapped in a paradox. To which I would only say: it's a novelist's duty to embrace contradiction.

Father David I'll wager you'd rather be embracing James MacMillan.

Mrs Anderton Well . . . given the choice. He is very good-looking.

A loud snip from Mrs Poole.

Father David *Attention! Pas devant la domestique.*

Mrs Anderton David!

Father David It's all right, Mother. Mrs Poole speaks very good French. In fact, she's a fellow Proustian.

Mrs Anderton I'm off. I'm clearly out of my depth.

She picks up her coat and looks at her watch.

Father David So soon?

Mrs Anderton I have to type up Paris. I've ordered a car. Thank you for the tea, Mrs Poole.

Flowers make such a difference. Bachelor bathroom apart, you've taken this place in hand, Mrs Poole. It feels less like a dusty mausoleum.

Father David Oh, we've kept the dust.

He and Mrs Poole look up at the chandelier.

Mrs Anderton Yes. It is a pity about the chandelier. But I know that's not negotiable. It still looks like something left over from a radical coup . . . which I suppose, metaphorically, it is.

There is a sudden silence between Mrs Anderton and her son.

My son was at Oxford in the sixties, Mrs Poole, when love and politics were inextricably linked.
Coups de foudres – coups d'états . . .
Inseparable.

Father David Didn't you have another bag, Mother?

Mrs Anderton Ah. In the kitchen. It's for you. More bottles for the bottle bank, I'm afraid, Mrs Poole. A rather good Armagnac. Offset by some of Valvona and Crolla extra virgin, which I was delighted to find in the pointless Duty Free. Nectar, both. The bag is rather vulgar but I'm assured it's recyclable.

Father David Goodbye, Mother. Sorry we didn't do lunch.

They kiss. Mrs Anderton looks at the rucksack.

Mrs Anderton Have a lovely picnic.

Father David More of a field trip.

Mrs Anderton Oh yes, I know. Pastoral care for the especially needy.

Mrs Poole snorts.
Father David releases the handle of his mother's bag.

Au revoir, Mrs Poole.

Mrs Poole *A bientôt*, Mrs Anderton.

Mrs Anderton I insist he spirits you over to the East Coast one day soon.
The Botanical Gardens are heaven in summer. Assuming there is one. Summer, I mean.

Mrs Anderton flashes her son a smile and exits, bag in train.

Mrs Poole I wish I had half your mother's energy.

Father David She always arrives and departs like a whirlwind, leaving everyone breathless in her wake.

Mrs Poole I like the sound of that Ayrshire composer.

Father David I'm sure you'll get to hear him soon enough. I'd guess a CD's already in the post.

Mrs Poole Your mother is a very generous woman.

Father David Yes. She is.
Chopin has a Scottish connection, you know. Late in his life, he came to Glasgow. He played at the Merchants' Hall.

Mrs Poole I bet he didn't get a full house.

Father David I refuse to be bullied out of the Nocturnes. I like them. They're hymn-like.

Mrs Poole Gluttons for sadness, Chopin fans. Bedwetters.

Father David laughs as he checks his rucksack.

Father David If it wasn't for Chopin, his countrymen would still be kicking up their heels in circles and baring their black teeth to the vodka jug.

Mrs Poole And this from a good socialist.

Father David Not in a long time.
I had a friend at Oxford who insisted that the state of mind produced by romantic music is an illusion. He said society, particularly English society, had too many of those. They needed shattering.
We'd stay up all night arguing about it.

Mrs Poole Sounds like a bit of a communist.

Father David More of an instinctive radical. A rebel with a cause. And of course just as romantic in his own way.

He came from Liverpool.

A slight pause.

I've always preferred Chopin to Bach.

Mrs Poole I'm no expert, but I'm sure that's wrong. Bach gets to the heart of things.

You might have to rectify that or else find another cleaner.

Father David A cleaner who likes Nocturnes?

Mrs Poole That's right. You're such a dangerous snob, Father David.

She bends to pick up a rose which she's dropped, but stops, clutching her back.

Father David No danger to you. You're the most gigantic snob I've ever met. I count it part of my good fortune to have come across you.

Mrs Poole Och, I intend to become much worse.

Father David Be my guest.

He picks up the flower.

Do you know the Empress Josephine's famous garden at Malmaison was almost entirely Galicia roses?

Mrs Poole Well, we must do better than the Empress Josephine, even if we only have our own poor soil to handle.

Father David Perhaps we should use something to help them along.

Mrs Poole Nothing chemical.

She rubs her back.

Father David Perhaps just a little to get them going.

Mrs Poole We could just as well put a banana peel in the soil. And some better manure. You can go out to the farms and get it free. (*Looking at his rucksack.*) We could go on a wee trip.

Father David Maybe you shouldn't bend down so much, Mrs Poole. Just until you're feeling better.

Mrs Poole There's nothing the matter with me.

Father David I bumped into Mr Poole. He said you'd not been feeling a hundred per cent.

Mrs Poole I've never been one for weddings. Jack's always glad of the excuse.

> *Mrs Poole suddenly interrupts her trimming to take a letter from her apron. She hands it to Father David. He reads it.*

I haven't told him. I don't want sympathy. And he'll just give me sympathy. That's not what I want. Do you know what I mean, Father?

Father David Yes, I think I do.

Mrs Poole They're trying things. But these drugs don't do anything.

> *He hands back the letter.*

Father David Give it time.

Mrs Poole Life's short.

Father David Come on, Mrs Poole.

Mrs Poole It's been coming to a head these last three months.
And God knows where I'm headed now.

Father David picks up his rucksack. He puts an arm round Mrs Poole.

That's just as good as a prayer.

'All the ladies in da house, yeh! yeh!
All the ladies in da house.'
    Lisa's wild hip-hop singing competes with the roar of the waves, as Mrs Poole and chandelier disappear, and they land on Ailsa Craig.

A huge seascape. Summer rain.

Mark and Lisa move forward together under their shared rain gear, like a strange animal.
    Father David, who has taken a waterproof from his rucksack, joins them.

SCENE FIVE

Father David What are you going on about, Lisa?

Lisa 'Am singin' my thing, Papa. All the babies go crazy when I get my milkshake on!

Father David You do come out with the most infernal rubbish.

Mark You are trippin', baby.

He now has his phone out and is texting.

Lisa Too right, nigga! All the ladies in da house!

Mark The only thing this crack whore knows about is hip-hop. She's the original Scottish coochie.

Lisa He's the one who's talking rubbish. You don't get crack around here. But we can fill you in on phenos, Papa.

Mark Phenobarbitone. What's their right name?

Lisa Dunno. Morphine something.

Mark And there's Codeine Phosphate Syrup. It's mad. Comes in a litre bottle off the shelf.

Lisa Diazepam they keep in drawers. Xanax comes in packets. And check out Ritalin. It's as good as E but speedier.

Mark But the drawers are usually locked . . .

Father David is silent.

Bugger it. Still nae signal.

Lisa Cheer up, Father.

Mark We're having a great day out, Father.

Father David That was the intention: to give a couple of gangsters something else to occupy their minds.

Mark Are there many boats doon there? Shipwrecks and that?

Father David Thousands. If it were winter, the waves would have gone right over our boat.
  Yes. You wouldn't have been showing off then.

Mark So it's just like one big graveyard.

Father David Sadly. Going back to before the Age of Improvement, when coal ships trailed these lanes. Merchant ships bound for the East Indies. And smugglers. The coast was bad for smugglers two or three hundred years ago.

Lisa Drugs?

Father David Brandy.

Mark Cool.

It must have been mad.
Like going oot in a boat in Vietnam in that film.

Father David Don't start talking about wars.

Mark Or the Falklands!
Knowing people could start shooting at you any minute. Totally mental. And you have a machine-gun rigged to get the bastards. Da-da-da-da. Daga-daga-daga-daga! Argies fallin about all over the place. Dumb fucks. Troops sorted them out. San Carlos Bay!

Father David You weren't even born.

Mark We're doin' it at school. Totally mad.

Lisa And the poor penguins. Mr Harris in History says hundreds of penguins got blown up doon there.

Mark Fuck penguins.

Lisa I think he fancies me.

Mark It's about sortin' out crappy dictators and stuff.

Lisa Mr Harris fancies me.

Mark Shove it, bitch!

Lisa Screw yoo, niggah!

Mark It's what needs doin' in the Middle East.
Is that not right? Eh?
Aw, come on Father. You hate Arabs just as much as us.

Father David I don't hate anyone, Mark. And you don't know the first thing about me.

Lisa Don't get eggy, Father. We're just havin' a buzz.

Father David Why do you say I hate Arabs?

Mark Because you let us talk nasty about them.

Father David That's got nothing to do with me.

Mark You like it. We're takin' a stand against evil. Fuck peace. You've got tae take a stand.

Father David To some extent, perhaps. But not always.

Mark It's like football. You want them tae win. You've got tae have your team, Father.

Lisa He would do anything for Celtic.

Father David Stop talking for a moment and listen.

The rain has stopped. The sound of the birds.

Lisa (*a whisper*) Are we the only people here?

Father David Yes. We're all alone here.

Mark Weird. That's weird. W-e-i-r-d.

Aware of an echo, Mark and Lisa can't resist exploiting it.
Lisa does her 'thang'.
Mark pays homage to Celtic: 'You'll never walk alone' etc.
He goes in search of a signal for his phone.
Lisa takes a swig of something fizzy.
She offers Father David. He refuses.

Lisa Not good enough for you, Father?

Father David I've brought my own.

He unscrews an apple-juice bottle that contains red wine.

Valpolicella.

Lisa That wine? Give us a swig.

He gives her the bottle. She takes a swig and hands it back.

How old are you, Father?

Father David Approaching sixty.

Lisa Sixty! That's mental.

So what's on the cards when you retire? Is there like a home for priests?

Father David No. You just go somewhere. There's always a lot in the world to be getting on with.

Lisa My dad hasn't worked since I was about two or three. Not since they closed Massey Ferguson.

Father David What does he do?

Lisa He does the Lotto.

Father David And what do you want to do?

Lisa I want to be, like, a make-up artist. For films and that. Or like on magazines.

You know, like where they go places with models and they put clothes on them and somebody does the make-up. That's me.

She looks out to sea.

I'll tell you something. I'm not hanging about over there.

Father David No? But I thought you weren't over-fond of foreigners.

Lisa Aye, but I don't care. I'd like to have lots of shoes.

Father David What else?

Lisa I want to go out and that. Buy a car. Gucci sunglasses. I want a pair of Gucci sunglasses.

Father David I'm sure you'll have that.

Lisa reaches for the wine.

Lisa Father, you have wasted your life, haven't you?

Father David I don't think so. I believe in God. That has been my life.

Lisa It can't be. You could have been having a good time and you've wasted it.

Father David That's not true, Lisa. We have different names for it, but I've lived according to my faith.

Lisa What's your name?

Father David Sorry?

Lisa Your real name. What is it?

Father David David . . . David Anderton.

Lisa So what's wrong with just being him?

Father David I am him.
Faith and good works. It's not your idea of a life, maybe. But it is mine.

Lisa Whatever.

They drink in silence from their respective bottles. Mark returns.

Mark The walls in there are thick with bird shit. Did people live there?

Father David Some people tried to. Two stone coffins were found in these caves. Apparently. Several years ago.

Mark 'Apparently', is it? The way you speak. The stuff you come out with.
You're so fucken posh, Father.

Father David Do forgive me. Perhaps I should annihilate my aitches and start saying 'ken' instead of 'know'. Or talking like one of your hip-hoppers.

Mark See what I mean? You're a riot.

Lisa (*finding the echo*) HE BELIEVES IN GOD.

She goes up to Mark.

36

Mark Freaky. And him a priest as well.

Father David (*also finding the echo*) HE IS THE SUPREME SPIRIT. HE IS INFINITE. HE IS AND ALWAYS WILL BE.

Mark Freaky!

Mark and Lisa stare at the sea.

Look at the water. You can see the fishing boats. It's totally mad. Everything's so wee from up here.

Father David It's the perspective. Like in a painting.

Mark Except we're real.

He puts an arm round Lisa. She leans on his shoulder.

Lisa Keeping it real, Father!

Father David Whatever.

Vaughan Williams's 'Fantasia on a Theme by Thomas Tallis'.
  Mark and Lisa. Silhouettes against a yellow sky.
  The chandelier. Mrs Poole is chopping rhubarb.

SCENE SIX

Mrs Poole Film music!
  Whatever next, Father?

Father David is texting on his new phone.

Father David You'll be interested to know the church organist's philistine views on Thomas Tallis are similar to your own.

Mrs Poole Wailing music for those who have trouble putting a smile on their faces.

Father David I've sacked him.

Mrs Poole That's a sure sign of age. It'll be me next. What am I doing with this rhubarb?

Father David Stewed. I thought we agreed on Monday. It's in the Fruit Book.

Mrs Poole Strictly speaking – as you might say – it's not actually a fruit.

Father David It's a pre-fruit.

Mrs Poole Semi-fruit.
It says here: 'The Greeks called this medicinal rhubarb, *rhu barbaron* because it reached them via foreigners – barbarians – down the river we call Volga and they call Rha.' The leaves were toxic.

Father David That's not the English kind. We only use pink stalks.

Mrs Poole Who's 'we'? Would that be the royal 'we'?

Father David Oh, shush.

More chopping. More texting.

Even the English kind has medicinal qualities. You should eat lots. Do you no end of good.

Mrs Poole I don't think rhubarb's the remedy.

Father David Maybe it's the bitterness. We always think bitterness is good for us.
Wouldn't you say?

Mrs Poole I don't know anything about it.

Father David It's true that rhubarb contains a lot of oxalic acid, and that can adversely affect the absorption of calcium and iron. You ought to watch that.

Mrs Poole stops chopping.

Mrs Poole Look, Father. I know you're trying to be helpful. I know you're trying to be kind. But you must stop talking to me about remedies and cures. It's offensive.

Father David I don't know what you mean.

Mrs Poole Yes, you do. In some way, it makes it easier for you, doesn't it?

It makes it easier for you to make light of what's happening and pretend I've got some . . . some stupid ailment. That's just the sort of person you are, Father David.

You really are quite English.

Father David Really?

Mrs Poole Just like that. The way you can say 'Really?'

It's English not to say things; to go on like you don't know things; to know how to put a name to a problem but not care how to solve it.

You think manners and conversation can get us round anything at all. But the truth is . . .

Father David Mrs Poole . . .

Mrs Poole The truth is, Father David, that I have cancer. Not just one but two kinds. That's that.

The truth is you will have to pay me off soon because I'm not going to be able . . .

Father David I understand.

Mrs Poole It's not your job to understand. It's not your job to make things smaller than they are.

Father David I am sorry if I have seemed to do that.

Mrs Poole You do it every time I see you and I expect more than that from you. I expect you to help me prepare.

I know you're afraid of death, Father. You fear death. You don't have any feeling for risk, that's your problem. It's because you haven't lived enough, Father.

39

A slight pause.

Father David That's not right, Mrs Poole. I have risked many things. A great many things. The person you see before you is the sum of his failures.

Mrs Poole There's no need to be so dramatic when you don't have to be. You're such an actor.

Father David Forgive me. I just want to help you.

Mrs Poole Well, if you want to help me, then help me. You've changed.

You don't sit and read now like you did when I first knew you.

It's good to see a man reading a book and improving himself. Jack would never do that. He's not stupid but he could never be at peace with himself for the time it takes to read a book. And you don't prepare for your Masses any more. You don't listen to your parishioners.

The people in the geriatric ward at Ravenspark say they haven't seen you for weeks.

Father David I've not gone anywhere, Mrs Poole.

Mrs Poole Have you not?

You've been such . . . such an inspiring person, Father David. Just in the way you lived. The way you appreciated things.

A slight pause.

And what's that hair gel doing on the bathroom shelf?

A text message comes through on Father David's phone.
 Mrs Poole clears up. Father David reads his text. The light on the chapel house fades.
 Men and women in the shadows.
 A loud ring-tone: 'You'll never walk alone'.
 Blue light through a boarded window. A peeling Guinness poster. Mark flicks his lighter.

Father David You should be in bed.

Mark (*singing*) It's Saturday night . . .

Father David Sunday morning.

Mark You should be on your knees.

He laughs.

I'm panelled.

Father David puts his phone in his pocket.

Father David Where are we?

Mark McNulty's Dalgarnock. Welcome to Provoland.

Father David What?

Mark The Provos. The Provisionals.

Father David Don't be ridiculous. You've never been to Ireland. What has the IRA got to do with you?

Mark My blood's been to Ireland. It started across the water, so don't go all English on me.

You have to watch yourself around here with all those Orange bastards.

Father David This is Scotland. Haven't you enough problems without importing fresh ones from over the water?

Mark Get a grip. You're a visitor here.

Father David The town's not that bad.

Mark Cop on. Five of the pubs here are Ulster Volunteer pubs.

I know your head's in the fucken clouds, Father. That's where it's supposed to be. But what kind of a place do you think this is? Do you actually know where you're living? Are you blind or what?

Father David Maybe I am. It's dark enough.

A slight pause.

When you're out by yourself around here, do you ever feel you're being watched?

Mark There's nobody here.

Mark lights a candle stuck in an old bottle. The shadowy figures have gone.

It's great here. It's the best place in the whole world.

Father David An empty pub? It's freezing. It smells of pee.

Mark Aye. People just take a slash if they need to. Have a few swigs of that.

He hands him a half-full bottle of vodka.

Father David Late licence?

Mark laughs.

Mark Use to be the Ardeer Arms. The windaes are boarded up but there's a padlock oot the back.

He takes off a shoe and reveals a key. It glints in the light.

Father David Why did it close?

Mark Dealers. It used to be a busy pub. Cabaret acts and that. Quiz nights. But the neds moved in, selling like, not just drugs but hard drugs. Then the brewery gave up. My mum and dad used to come down here. Everybody on the estate came down.

Father David So it was busy?

Mark Packed Friday and Saturday nights. Couples like. Married couples. All that shite.

There's better pubs in town. There were a good few stramashes in here. The piss-artist who's married to your housekeeper . . . Poole. Jack Poole – he once threw a full pint of Guinness into the puggie – fruit machine.

Father David Did he really?

Mark A few of us come here when we're bunkin' off school.

At night, though, it's usually just me on my own. That's when I like it best. Pure magic.

Father David The bliss of solitude . . .

A silence between them.

Mark Do you like pubs?

Father David I used to. When I was a student.

Mark Were you clever at being a student?

Father David Not especially.

Mark Did you always get top marks?

Father David I think I was more interested in pubs. One loses sight of pubs.

Mark Does one?

They smile. The vodka bottle is empty.

Father David It's still freezing.

Mark puts on his shoe.

Mark Got any beer?

He snuffs the candle.

The chandelier is lit for the first time.
  It casts a shadow on the centre of the rug.

Father David (*off*) Is your father still not working?

Mark (*off*) Retired. Told ye. He's a fat bastard.

Father David (*off*) Be kind, Mark.

They come into the room.

He gets depressed, doesn't he, your father?

Mark How do you know?

Father David It's quite a small parish.

Mark looks up at the chandelier.

Mark Job came up recently. He couldnae do it. He was 'para'.

Father David Paralytic?

Mark No, stupid. Paranoid.
Cool carpet. English?

Father David Persian.

Mark Iraq!

Father David Iran.

Mark It's got blood on it.

Father David What?

Mark Black blood.

Father David That's a shadow, stupid.

Mark Looks like blood tae me.

Father David Paranoia.

Mark Paralytica. Where's the beer?

Father David No beer, sorry. Only wine.

Father David goes to the kitchen.

Mark If you've got Cola, we could mix it with the wine and get some Jesus juice going.

Father David (*off*) Just wine.

Mark Any roach material?

Father David (*off*) No.

Mark Any CDs?

Father David (*off*) Hundreds.

Mark One'll do.

He produces a collection of drugs from his pocket. He stacks them like a child's building blocks.
Father David has put on a Beatles album. Mark winces.

You didnae have to take the disc out.

Father David, now in his shirtsleeves, brings wine, corkscrew, glasses and the CD case.

Father David Have you heard of the Beatles?

Mark Not lately.

Father David What are these?

Mark Scooby snacks.

Mark uses the small knife of the corkscrew to cut up pills on the CD case.

Got a business card?

Father David looks in his wallet and pulls one out.

'Social Services Department'. Wicked.

He tears off a piece.

Don't worry. You can still see her number.

Father David opens and pours the wine.

There you go.

*He has chopped some pills in half and is making a
joint.*

Show me your tongue.

*Father David hesitantly complies.
Mark puts half a pill on his tongue.
Father David swallows.
Mark hands him his glass.*

Amen.

Father David Please don't.

Mark Just gub it down.

*Mark swallows his half. They drink more wine.
Mark takes off his jacket. He starts to dance.
Father David sways.
They sway together in time to the music.*

I'm fucked up.

*More wine etc.
As another album track starts, Mark lights his joint.
He lies on the rug, smoking.*

Bet between us, we could make this thing fly, Father.

Father David stares down at him.

Father David We need some water and a change of tune.

He goes out.

Mark Nothin' crappy. Nothin' by auld geezers wi' specs.

Father David (*off*) Hold on.

He puts on some Delius.

46

Mark What's this?

Father David (*off*) The sound of a genius.

Mark Sounds like a total loofah.

Father David returns with a bottle of water.

Father David Just listen and don't be a moron.

Mark This music would do your nut in.

He laughs. Father David sits beside him on the rug.

Father David He was born in Yorkshire, Delius.

Mark Good for him. What does it matter where anybody's from?

Father David It matters.
I went to school there.

Mark Top skunk. Want a puff?

They sink back on the rug.

Father David Sad about your dad.

Mark He's a sad fuck. Off his face half the time.
Been on the government cheese for years but still says he's a worker.
He thought he had a job one time. He would come down early like, every morning for ages, put on his working boots and go out into the front garden. Completely out of it.
He would bring a shovel sometimes and start digging. The fucker would stand in his boxer shorts and his big tackety boots talking shite about tea breaks and overtime and the van coming to pick him up.

Father David That's very sad.

Mark It's mental.

Father David Sad not to work when you're able and willing.

Mark You're a peach. He doesn't want tae work. You kiddin'? He wouldnae work if you paid him.

Well, maybe if you paid him a lot. He's 'para'. Always been like that.

Father David Sad.

Mark The other week he buried the ironing board oot the back. My ma didn't know what was happening. He was oot there wi' that spade, diggin' a hole for hours. He buried the ironing board and the drainin' thing off the sink. Then he sat on the back step, rolling cigarettes. Completely sparkled.

A slight pause.

At least he's got Sky.

They both find this funny.
Father David rests his head on Mark's shoulder.

Father David You don't mind, do you?

Mark Knock yourself out.

He leans over and kisses Mark's cheek. Then his mouth.

Cut it out.

Father David By all means.

He takes his hand.

Mark This is mental.

Father David Yes. That's what it is. Mental.

They lie together in the shadow of the chandelier.

Delius has stopped.

Birdsong.
A shaft of early light.
Mrs Poole comes in with two plastic bags.
She sees the sleeping pair. She sighs. Then leaves.
Men and women silhouetted against the morning
sky. The sound of a single drum.

Act Two

A drum roll leads into the sound of a flute band.
   Slowly, out of the dark, the men and women of West Ayrshire. Silhouettes against an evening sky.

The chandelier is switched on.
   The band cuts out. Schumann takes over.
   Father David, a white-napkinned bottle of wine in each hand, stands above his table, elaborately laid for five.

SCENE ONE

Father David *Bon appétit!*

   His guests come forward.
      Bishop Gerard, the guest of honour.
      Father Damian, a young priest.
      Angela Path, director of Dalgarnock Social Services.
       And Mr McCallum, Headmaster of St Andrew's Academy, who is drunk.

Bishop Goodness me, David. What is this you're giving us?

Father David Burgundian fish stew. A favourite recipe.

Father Damian *Placements*, is it?

Father David Yes, indeed.
   Gerard – head of the table, *bien sûr*!
   The lady is over here.

   He indicates Angela's chair.

Angela (*laughing*) Not exactly boy–girl–boy–girl,
Father . . .

Father Damian snorts.

Father David Nor is your esteemed presence mere
tokenism, Madame Director.
  I regard it as my bounden duty to wrest you from your
hotbed of feminism, for one evening at least.

Angela I'm not sure I'm dressed for a social experiment.

Mr McCallum You look very nice.

He attempts to pull out her chair.

Angela Why, thank you, kind sir. We seem to be the only
two out of uniform.

Mr McCallum School uniform is the bane of my life.

They take their seats.

Father David And I'm afraid I'll have to insist on you
drinking the wine in the prescribed order.
  I'm feeling very bossy tonight.
  And no mixing the wine in your glasses either.

He pours.

These are from vineyards right next to each other.

Father Damian I'm not a wine man. You couldn't manage
a wee whisky?

Father David Ice?

Father Damian You're joking, man. We don't have ice in
our whisky up here. This is Scotland.

Father David Oh.

Father Damian Talk about sacrilegious.

Mr McCallum A lovely glass of wine, that. Not too dry.

Father David Each is from the same region as the recipe for the stew.

An Aligoté from Meursault, and a rather nice Clos de Vougeot.

Mr McCallum (*embarrassed*) Well. You certainly know your way round a menu, Father David.

Bishop 'Twas ever thus.

Father David leaves to fetch the whisky.
Light has faded on the men and women.
The Schumann track has ended.

Father Damian Perhaps you should introduce wine tasting to the school curriculum, Mr McCallum.

Mr McCallum The syllabus is gey crowded as it is, Father Damian. I think educating their palates will have to wait.

Bishop Would that come under the heading of sociological innovation, Angela?

Father Damian Or substance abuse?

Laughter.

Angela Perhaps Mr McCallum could sneak it in under Citizenship.

The Social Services Department is always open to new ideas.

Bishop Some might say that, since you took it over, it's ventilated a few too many already.

Angela Like you, Bishop, we do our best to keep up with the times.

Father David has returned with a bottle of Laphroaig
and a crystal tumbler, which he places before Father
Damian.

Father Damian That'll do.

The others watch as he pours himself a generous amount.

Sláinte!

'Cheers', 'Santé', 'Happy days' etc.
The Bishop says grace. They sup their stew.

Angela What a divine concoction! You can taste the sea. Is that not what they say, Bishop?

Bishop You'll know better than me, I'm sure.
It's interesting, you know, when it comes to the sea. I've always been quite nervous of it. Of course, the gospels have a great deal to say about it. You think of Galilee, and the Apostles out there with Christ. I get the message of all that of course, but I never liked the actual water myself. I think the ocean is a vastly overrated thing.

Angela Well, perhaps if you were to walk on it, Bishop . . . but I don't know if you've quite got there yet.

Cordial laughter.

Bishop I'm willing to see it as a family thing. My people came from County Monaghan. That's a landlocked county. We don't have a strong sense of the sea.

Father David That's a pity, Gerard. The sea is a great fund of miracles. And we have crossed a great many seas to where we are now.

Mr McCallum True enough.

Father David And we are fisher priests.

Father Damian But you need to beware what you catch.

He and Angela laugh.

Bishop Untoward, Father Damian.

Father Damian Sorry, My Lord. You can't get far in this world without a wee joke, sure you can't.

Father David Well, I grew up by the sea.

Father Damian In England.

Father David pours more wine and addresses Mr McCallum.

Father David I think people who grew up by the sea have a different feeling about nationhood. You have the country at your back, your own country. But, facing out to sea, you tend to think of other countries. The world beyond.

Bishop And you feel a kinship with other nations, don't you, David?

Father David Well, I have cared for them a great deal in the past, Gerard, as you know.
  Perhaps one looks more inwardly as time goes on.

Angela You don't want to become complacent. We're in a strange place just now, with every country feeling their sovereignty matters above all others. I mean, we live in a time when, for example, an American life is taken to be more valuable than any other sort of life, especially a Muslim one.

Mr McCallum Surely not.

Angela Every time. Now you men like to talk about the sanctity of life . . .

Bishop Oh, heavens. Let's not get started on that this evening.

Angela No, forgive me, sir, you all bang on about the sanctity of life and so does the Christian Right in America. You want everything to be born that can be born, am I right?

But when you're talking about actual lives – people already living – the Americans have a rather different notion. What notion of the sanctity of life informed carpet-bombing in Iraq?

Father Damian Or the blatant disregard for civilian casualties in Afghanistan?

Bishop The Church agrees with you. The Holy Father agrees. We are not always in a position to direct national feelings but the substance of your comment is not offensive to a Catholic ear.

Mr McCallum (*extending his glass to Father David*) Aye, but change is on the way!

Angela Is it? The new regime is already talking about making this century the next American Century.

Mr McCallum Och, I know that America's the current big bogeyman, but every country since the year dot has had an eye out for its own interests. Scotland's no exception. Look at our colonial incursions into India and Africa.

Father David When I was young . . .

Bishop Ah, when you were young . . .

Father David When I was young, we were moved to oppose colonialism or capitalism or whatever the jargon was. We wanted America to leave the people of Vietnam to build their own society. But now? There are leaders in the Middle East harming their own people. It's a nest of caliphs. And they want nuclear weapons. People who are not merely sentimental in their politics will see that we must gather our forces to prevent them. You've got to take a stand. It's a dirty job.

Father Damian That's immoral. We don't have the right.

Angela I didn't realise I'd been invited to the Republican National Convention.

Father Damian Nobody here agrees with what you're saying.

Mr McCallum He's got a point.

You get sick of the sound of liberal knee-jerkers jerking off.

Father David History is imperfect, and so is America. But the world is too dangerous now.

We may each of us have to trade in a little of our idealism for the sake of the new realities.

Father Damian The fact is we have joined the Americans, trying to capitalise on a situation, trying to get a foothold in the Middle East, trying to protect – to expand their own interest. America used the thing in New York as an excuse for an invasion and if you can't see that you're blind.

Bishop David, we must not ignore what our vocation tells us. It tells us to understand the hate in the eyes of our enemies. We have not sought to understand ourselves or them. America simply closed its eyes and pulled the trigger and we followed them. And in the process, we have not lessened hatred. On the contrary, we have increased it and made it noble in the eyes of millions.

Father David It was always noble in their eyes.

Bishop You don't believe that.

Father David We have arrived at different places, Gerard. Out of the past, we have come to different places. My view has not changed, or not much. The vista has changed, and what we are looking at is not the same as Vietnam.

Father Damian It does the Church no favours that we should be harbouring people who think such things, support such hatred.

Mr McCallum 'Harbouring'?

Father Damian The difference between now and the past, the past you have turned your back on, is that – in spite of the recent gush of euphoria – America has now irrevocably forced the world into being dominated by primitive notions of good and evil.

Father David You're talking about our creed.

Father Damian Rubbish.

Father David Really? I don't think so. We spend our days being rather certain about where goodness lies and evil prevails.

Angela It's no basis for a foreign policy.

Father David It's the Church's policy on everything, Angela.
    I rather think Father Damian finds himself imprisoned in a contradiction.

Bishop Scotland has always been a socialist country. And some forms of wisdom are hard to import. Perhaps the English, perhaps the Americans, have lost some sense of subtlety when it comes to handling good and evil. We see it differently here in Scotland.

Father David Gerard, in a town like this, with its history of bigotry and Orangeism and everything else, you're going to give us a lecture on the fair-mindedness of the Scottish people? About their working-class camaraderie? Their feeling for the international poor? Their native opposition to economic self-interest? Their inclusiveness?

Mr McCallum That's a good one!

Father David Last week a girl from Glasgow had her throat cut in broad daylight for wearing a football scarf. Two asylum-seekers were thrown off the top of a block of flats, not ten miles from here. So please spare me your homily about the glory of the tribe.

Mr McCallum Oh, the tribe!

Mr McCallum knocks over his glass. A pause. Father David receives a text on his phone.

Angela Let me.

She starts to clear up. Father Damian lends a hand. Mr McCallum staggers out.

Mr McCallum Excuse me.

Father David is reading his text.

Angela (*clearing up*) I've always thought it ironic that your Pope has so much time for the Virgin Mary. You'd have thought her being of the female persuasion might have bothered him.

Father Damian (*stacking plates*) What are you saying? The Church doesn't approve of women?

Angela You prefer saints. Bless the Pope, but he's much more understanding of celestial bodies than he is of women's.

Father Damian Polytechnic speak.

They continue to argue light-heartedly as dishes, glasses etc. are taken off.
Father David continues to stare at his phone.

Father David It doesn't matter.

Bishop What did you say?

Father David Oh, nothing.

Bishop Do you ever hear anything from your old monks? The ones from Ampleforth.

Father David I don't. I never hear of them.

Bishop Our host went to a very good school.

Father David It was a long time ago.

Bishop A famous one. Down in Yorkshire.

Father David That's all in the past.

Father Damian I don't think so. You still have a touch of the lobster salad about you.

An awkward silence.

Bishop Well, that's certainly been to our benefit, this evening.
We thank you, David, for such an ample supper.

'I'll say', 'Delicious', etc.

And a frank exchange of views is always an invigorating thing.

Angela I hope so.

Father Damian (*folding his napkin ostentatiously*) And we're always too busy with practical things to harp on about good and evil.

Angela laughs.

Bishop Let an old Glasgow hand have the final word.
It is the modern world: we do not have all the answers, but in Scotland I believe it is our oldest habit to live and let live.

The heavily amplified sound of a heartbeat.
The chapel house and its guests disappear.
Jack Poole pushes on his wife in a wheelchair.
She is pale and has a newspaper on her lap.
She presses an egg-shaped object.

*The heartbeat is replaced by an equally overamplified
soundtrack of seabirds and surf.*

A sea view from a hospital window.

*Father David is holding a paperback and a bunch of
red roses.*

SCENE TWO

Father David No music?

Mrs Poole Fed up with music.

Father David That's a pity.

Mrs Poole Sometimes you just want to cut to the chase.
    This is a very handy object. It makes me think of
outside.
    That was 'Soothing Heartbeat' followed by 'Ocean
Beach'.
    I'm saving 'Babbling Brook' and 'Alpine Sunrise' for
after lunch.

A slight pause.

Saumon poêlé au vin blanc de la Loire.

Father David *Ce n'est pas vrai!*

Mrs Poole Jack brought salmon steaks from Somerfield's.
There's a bottle of white in the fridge.

Father David Sorry. I can't stay.

Another pause.

Mrs Poole (*to her husband*) These'll be needing water.

Mr Poole takes the roses from Father David.

Father David Thank you, Mr Poole.

Mr Poole Jack.

He leaves with the flowers.

Father David Your hair's different.

Mrs Poole It's a wig.

Father David Of course.
  I brought you a book.

Mrs Poole What is it?

Father David An old one of my mother's. *Parliament of Crows.*

Mrs Poole What's it about?

Father David Oh, the usual. Everything and nothing. It's about the lengths people go in order to remain unhappy.

A slight pause.

Mrs Poole Your mother's good at what she does.

Father David Indeed.

Mrs Poole She's been very good to me. You know I only accepted this private room because I didn't want to offend her kindness. Jack was against it.

Father David I hope I haven't frightened Mr Poole away.

Mrs Poole He's fine. There's a pub across the road.

Father David hands her the book.

Father David It's a novel about the last years of Fanny Osborne, the woman who married Robert Louis Stevenson. He was the one with the famous stories, of course, but Fanny had her stories too, secret ones.
  Her life was in some ways more interesting than his, according to my mother.

Mrs Poole I'll be glad to read the book rather than all this stuff.

Father David The paper? No, it's not cheering.

Mrs Poole Bloody shambles. Why don't we just leave people in peace?

Father David Because some people don't know what peace is.

Mrs Poole And you a good socialist.

Father David That old chestnut. I'm praying things will turn out better – for everyone.

Mrs Poole That'll be useful.

Father David Don't be sarcastic.

Mrs Poole Well, don't be shallow. I tell you, Father David, I think you're getting more like those warmongers by the second.

Father David By the decade, perhaps.

Mrs Poole puts the book in the pocket of her chair.

Mrs Poole You have more faces than the town clock.

Father David I think you expect too much of me, Mrs Poole.

Mrs Poole You are repulsive.

Father David I beg your pardon.

Mrs Poole You are a coward. A hypocrite.

Father David Mrs Poole, please . . .

Mrs Poole What do you know of the world? Where have you been? Had you any life at all, ever?

Father David I've had some.

Mrs Poole Where was that? Oxford University? With your Chopin and your commie friend?

Staying up all night under your chandelier . . . on your Persian rug!

Don't make me laugh.

A slight pause.

Father David I've never spoken to anyone about my life.

Mrs Poole And no wonder. There is no life. Nothing. It's all invisible with your kind. You're just like those warmongers. You believe in whatever suits you at the time.

Father David Mrs Poole, you're not well.

Mrs Poole Aye. But I know what my illness is. What's yours?

Father David Mrs Poole . . .

Mrs Poole All this talk of morality.

She brandishes the newspaper.

What morality? It's all lies. Lies. People just lie about what they do and who they are and you are just . . . you are just part of it.

She flings the newspaper across the room.

Father David You're angry because you're ill. I perfectly understand . . .

Mrs Poole Oh, please. Don't make a hero of yourself every time.

Father David Mrs Poole. Let me help you.

Mrs Poole I saw you with him.

You desecrated that house. And I loved it there.

Father David It will always be there.

Mrs Poole You are a fool, Father. And I feel sorry for you. I really do. You don't know what you've done.

You know so much. Except loyalty. You know nothing about loyalty, Father.

Father David The way you talk. You didn't learn that from your husband.

Mrs Poole I learnt it from you.

I didn't want to have the same disease as Jack's mother died of. I really didn't want that.

I wanted to show him I was better.

Father David You are better.

Mrs Poole See how easy it comes to you, Father. You didn't even know the woman.

She picks up the sound machine.
Mr Poole has entered behind her, with the red roses.
He is followed by a young, uniformed policeman.

You're just like this. You sound perfectly natural, but you are not natural at all.

Policeman Are you David Anderton?

Mrs Poole turns to see them both.

Is that correct?

Father David Yes. That's right . . . I am David Anderton.

Mrs Poole presses the sound machine wildly,
occasioning a cacophony of amplified sound, as she
wheels herself off.
The policeman and Mr Poole disappear.
The sea view is replaced by silhouetted men and
women.
Their shouts of 'Dirty Fenian Bastard, 'Dirty
English Cunt', 'Fucking Child Molester', 'Fucking
Beast' etc. build to a crescendo.

64

A litany of hatred. Then a huge cry in unison:
'Paedophile!'
The chandelier crashes to the floor.
The silhouetted men and women are replaced by
PEEDAPHILE *scrawled in giant red letters.*
Father David is dabbing his forehead with a blood-
stained baby's bib.

SCENE THREE

Father David (*surveying the damage*) Good Lord.

Mr Poole comes in with Father David's keys.

Mr Poole Jesus Christ.
Here's your car keys. You'll be okay from here. You'll
need to get the lock fixed.

Father David I'm most grateful, Mr Poole. Why don't I
make some tea?

Mr Poole No, you're awright. This is Anne's place of
work. It wouldnae be right.
I've never been where she works. She wouldnae like it.

Father David Well, thank you very much for coming to
my aid.

Mr Poole It's a rough business.

Mr Poole leaves.
Father David makes a half-hearted attempt to
straighten the rug. He gives up and sits on it.
After a few moments, the Bishop appears.

Bishop Dear God.
Are you all right? The front door was open.

No response.

It's Gerard.

Father David Yes. Good afternoon, Bishop.

Bishop How are you?

Father David Quite chipper for someone who was charged yesterday. Would you like some tea?

Bishop I don't want anything. Are you really all right?

Father David I'm not a hundred per cent. But don't worry. I won't be inflicting any further wounds. A kind woman gave me her baby's bib. Do you think she'll want it back?

He leaves for the kitchen.

Bishop Father Brendan tells me you're refusing counsel.

Father David (*off*) I'm not guilty. I'm not apologising to the families and hanging my head before the tabloids.

He returns with a plaster, which he has difficulty opening.

Bishop Look, the boy's fifteen years old. He was . . . here . . . at seven o'clock in the morning. Drugs were involved. He's given a statement. So have others. His father's on the warpath.

Father David (*indicating his forehead*) Yes. I should imagine this represents a fairly accurate encapsulation of his father's views. It seems to me I'm currently more victim than perpetrator.

It was not sexual assault, Gerard. Not to my mind.

Bishop And what is your mind?

Father David finally succeeds in sticking the plaster to his head.

I took a chance bringing you to this diocese. I went against advice to bring you from England. You know what, David: the Bishop of Lancaster gave you a questionable reference. He said you'd spent nearly twenty years being an excellent administrator and a poor pastor. He said you'd organised a cabal – that was his word – of classical music lovers and wine tasters. Wine tasters! That's what your ministry at Blackpool consisted of in the mind of your Bishop.

Father David So why didn't he fire me?

Bishop For the same reasons I didn't. Because he thought you were intelligent and because we're short of priests.

Father David I'm grateful.

Bishop No, God strengthen us, I don't think you are.
  All those years ago in Rome, when I met you at the English school, you were full of zeal for the Church. Things were changing. It was our time, and you had the character to meet all the challenges. Is not that right? And what happened to you? You ended up frittering away your vocation, reading paperbacks and cooking fish.

Father David I never had the character, Gerard. I was just a lonely young man. I think you knew that.

Bishop Don't tell me what I knew! You had a calling. You had faith in God. And I had faith in you. How dare you deny that now?

Father David Nevertheless, my faith was built on the wrong foundation. It was built on . . . the wrong things.

Bishop There are no wrong things to build faith on.

Father David I'm sorry, but there are.

Bishop What are you saying?

Father David I'm saying I think I used the Church. It was a beautiful hiding place.
  I'm sure it has been for others.

Bishop You're having a crisis. I've seen it before. You need to retreat and examine your faith. You need a holiday.

Father David My life has been a holiday.

A slight pause.

Bishop And you bring this to my door.

Father David I'm sorry for that. I truly am. Please believe that, Gerard.
And I'm sorry to the parishioners and to God.

Bishop Maybe you've always had a touch of the victim. I remember showing you round the chapel and the room where Galileo was interrogated. The house next to the Church. You wanted to stand there for ever, you said. You were full of all your Oxford questions. Book questions. Faith questions.

Father David I have always been interested in the telescope.

Bishop No, David. You were playing the part of Galileo. One of the friars was telling us about the Dominicans' interrogation of him, and you were transfixed, mouthing the words along with him. You've always been an actor, David. And an actor will always want to play a part.

Father David My confusions were genuine.

Bishop But why now? Why has it all come back now?

Father David Our lives are liable to catch up with us, Gerard.

A silence between them.

Bishop This is only egotism. The great destroyer. We can fix this.

Father David How?

Bishop Inside the Church. We have experience and we can solve the problem in our own way. That is our strength.

Father David It is a criminal matter. That is how it will be fixed.

Bishop Don't misunderstand me. I have already asked the police if it was okay to speak with you. I am not interested in covering anything up.

Father David Heaven forfend.

Bishop You are not considering your parishioners. Their faith is in your hands and we cannot suffer this to happen. David, think again. Cleave to the love of the faithful. You have never loved them. You took your role seriously, but only as a role.

Father David I did not set out to possess their hearts.

Bishop That is a wicked statement. Is that one of your aesthetic defences? Because art will not defend you now.

Father David Sadly not.

Bishop You're not thinking straight. No matter what you say, the public will crucify you.

Father David I appreciate all the efforts you've made for me, Gerard. But I am my own Judas. My own Pontius Pilate. I kissed the boy and will fight the matter in my own way.

Bishop It will be all politics and newspapers. And you're bad at politics.
    You know nothing about the papers up here. You don't understand what people will try to make of this.

Father David I must take my chances.

Bishop I will cut you adrift.

Father David As you must.

Bishop You don't know where you're heading.

Father David 'If one does not know to which port one is sailing, no wind is favourable.' Seneca.

Bishop And this is the kind of remark that will destroy you.

Father David What happens now?

Bishop I must place you on administrative leave. You will leave the rectory by noon tomorrow. We could arrange a place for you at Dirrans Monastery.

Father David That won't be necessary.

Bishop Look, David, think about what I'm saying. He that yields to reproof shows understanding. A little humility would help you now.

Father David A little late in the day for that, is it not?

Messiaen's 'Oiseaux Exotiques'.
   The Water of Leith.
   Trees. A bench.
   Father David is walking with his mother in the early evening. He carries an Edinburgh Festival concert programme.

SCENE FOUR

Father David Birds were the first musicians.

He opens the programme.

Messiaen was taking over from Debussy.
   Listen to this, Mother: 'What is left for me, but to seek out the true, lost face of music somewhere off in the

forest, in the fields, in the mountains or on the seashore, among the birds.'

He hands his mother the programme.

Mrs Anderton Messiaen's birds sounded more real than the real thing.
I love the Festival. I love the word. Particularly when qualified by 'international'.

They have found a bench and sit.

And 'Edinburgh'.
What was the name of the second piece?

Father David *'Trois petites liturgies de la Présence Divine'*.

Mrs Anderton I think I preferred the birds one.

Father David Me too. More religious.

Mrs Anderton More celestial.
They were very young, weren't they, those singers?

Father David They were lovely.

*They listen to the sounds of the evening.
Messiaen's birds replaced by the real thing.*

You happy with your new book?

A slight pause.

Mrs Anderton They'll love it in France.

Father David Is there sex?

Mrs Anderton Buckets.

Another pause.

Most of it takes place at night.
There's an outpouring of devastating emotion on the headland. You know the sort of thing.

Slight pause.

The usual, I'm afraid.

Father David I'm sure your readers wouldn't have it any other way.

Mrs Anderton One seeks to make all the sexual encounters vaguely reflective of the national scene.

Father David Perfect.

Mrs Anderton They are entertainments.

Father David That is the best one can hope for.

Mrs Anderton Did you love that boy?

Father David Which boy?

Mrs Anderton The one from Ayrshire. I know you loved Conor.

Father David Ah.

Mrs Anderton What is it?

Father David It's so strange hearing someone speak his name, after all this time.

Mrs Anderton Conor is still the central matter in all this? After all these years?

Father David nods slowly.

Father David He was real, Mother.
He was the answer to the question of how to live and what to do.

Mrs Anderton Two questions.

Father David With a single answer.
There was a stone bridge and some trees. I kept the taxi waiting.

The driver said most of them had been cut down by the furniture industry.

They said it was the spot where he died.

I never saw the body. I never went back to Liverpool. I never spoke to his mother and father. I didn't attend the funeral. I never took my degree. And the years have only enlarged the space made by his absence. But.

Mrs Anderton What?

Father David Perhaps, if he'd lived, we would have lived too closely and learnt to hate the smallness of each other's habits, needs, doubts . . .

Conor had the grace to lose his life at a moment of unimpeachable promise. But we might have come to hate each other, to see only faults and bad faith.

Mrs Anderton But you don't believe that.

Father David It comforts me to think so. He lost his life before his love of life, or of me, was tested, so becoming one of those golden boys of Oxford his radical credentials forbade him to admire.

Yes.

Not falling down in a foreign field at Ypres, not dying of consumption on a wormy bench, but growing drowsy, it seems, in the foothills of the Chilterns and crashing his beloved second-hand Triumph Herald on the main road outside High Wycombe.

Mrs Anderton You've let the past catch up with you.

Father David The Ayrshire boy's name is Mark. He's very young. I tried to kiss him one night.

It was just my own stupidity. I don't think the boy cared that much, but I think his father has a score to settle and it's all quite sad.

Mrs Anderton You kissed the young man?

Father David Yes, I got drunk with him. We took other stuff. I definitely kissed him and held his hand. He must have told his father. I don't know how it came out, but the poor man hasn't worked for years. Perhaps this gives his life some focus. Anyway, he's taking a stand. And the whole parish wants to kill me. They want some sport.

Mrs Anderton Don't be dismissive. You knew what kind of community it was down there for a Catholic priest.

Father David And they say I'm English.

Mrs Anderton Oh dear.

Father David And they think I'm posh.

Mrs Anderton And now you're up on some molesting charge?

Father David It's not called that, but yes: sexual assault.

Mrs Anderton You'll have spoken to that nice advocate Hamilton? You intend to fight?

Father David Yes.

Mrs Anderton For your career?

Father David No, that's gone. Perhaps it should have gone a long time ago.

Mrs Anderton But what about your friend – your God?

Father David You're so mercilessly practical, Mother. You won't like me for saying this, but I believe God is present in all this too.

Mrs Anderton I see. Well, that's the sort of thing you people say. He's never caused anything but trouble in the world before now.

Father David Shush.

Mrs Anderton And what does Hamilton say?

74

Father David He said the boy's a thug. He says it was a kiss of affection, a way of saying goodnight.

Mrs Anderton And you can go with that?

Father David I don't think so. I want to tell the truth.

Mrs Anderton Well, this is Scotland. That might seriously hamper your chances of a getting a fair hearing.

Father David Be serious.

Mrs Anderton You want to tell the truth?

Father David If I know it, yes. And if I can. I don't mind saying I fell for him. I admit to being the most stupid person on earth. But I'm not a paedophile or anything of that sort and I won't agree to it being called assault.

Mrs Anderton In this area, the law is not built for subtleties. Or at least the public nowadays is not minded for subtlety. I'd hang on to Hamilton, if I were you.

Father David I'm guilty of something – of many things – perhaps – but not of what they say.

A text comes through on Father David's phone.

Father David Mrs Poole.

Mrs Anderton I shouldn't have thought texting was quite her style.

Father David Since her illness, she's become addicted to technology . . .
    They've burned down the rectory – and set fire to my old car.

Mrs Anderton The times are hysterical.

She takes her son's hand.

Don't feel guilty about thoughts. Don't feel guilty about feelings. Just look to what you actually did.

Father David My actions were minimal. It's all the other stuff that matters.

My vocation has run its course. I need a new life.

Mrs Anderton Or an old one.

Father David Perhaps.

Mrs Anderton But the court won't bother with that. They'll be dealing with the image of a lascivious priest. The town will be baying for blood. They watch a lot of television, one presumes.

Father David Some very good people live there.

Mrs Anderton I'm sure. But every small town loves a scapegoat.

Father David They've been seeking scapegoats in that town for five hundred years.

Mrs Anderton Well, they've got one now.

Sounds of microphones being tested.

The Water of Leith becomes a huge flickering screen – the 'video link' – which finally comes into focus and bears the logo: KILMARNOCK SHERIFF COURT.

Mrs Fraser, the Procurator Fiscal, Mr Hamilton, for the defence, and Father David, now without his dog collar.

Mr Dorran and Mrs Poole are seated to one side.

SCENE FIVE

The Clerk (*unseen*) Are you David Anderton?

No response.

Is that correct?

Father David Yes, that's right.

He stands.

I am David Anderton.

The Clerk It is alleged that in the early hours of 11 July this year you did sexually assault Mark McNulty in the chapel house of the Church of St John Ogilvie in the town of Dalgarnock. How do you plead?

Father David Not guilty.

The Sheriff is also unseen.
His amplified voice booms from the back of the auditorium.

Sheriff I would ask you to speak with more volume. Your voice is of a tincture we don't often hear in this environment.

Father David Fine.

Sheriff Speak up.

Father David That's fine.

Sheriff Quite so.
We gather you are a graduate of Oxford University.

Father David Alas, not a graduate, Your Lordship. But, yes. I was a student there.

Sheriff Which college?

Father David Balliol, Your Lordship.

Sheriff Ah. 'Never apologise, never explain.' Benjamin Jowett, was it not? The head of Balliol?

Father David Yes, The Master of Balliol.

Sheriff Proceed, Mrs Fraser.

Father David sits with his barrister.
Mr Dorran is walking forward.

A spotlight hits him.
The Procurator Fiscal rises.

Mrs Fraser Mr Dorran, how long have you been teaching at St Andrew's Academy?

Mr Dorran Nearly twenty years.

Mrs Fraser And over that time, have you had much to do with the religious aspects of the children's education?

Mr Dorran A great deal. As a music teacher, I've always thought it important to help with hymns and that, to try and increase a child's faith, if you like, with the right music.

Mrs Fraser And so you would say you had the trust of the children and their parents when it came to religious education?

Mr Dorran Oh, aye. I often work in partnership with parents to improve the chances of the children getting a Catholic education.

Mrs Fraser And you have seen a number of priests in the parish then?

Mr Dorran Two or three, yes. Over the years.

Mrs Fraser And what did you think of David Anderton's contribution to your efforts in that regard?

Mr Dorran Well, obviously, at first, he's well-educated and that, so we were glad to have a parish priest who cared about teaching as a profession. He helped out very well at the school a couple of times. But Father David had a character problem. Is it okay to say that?

Sheriff Go on.

Mr Dorran He had what I'd call a natural ability to wind people up.

Sheriff A what?

Mr Dorran I said he wound people up, Your Honour.

Sheriff I'm not Your Honour, I'm My Lord.

Mr Dorran Sorry, sir. He wound all the staff up. He got snobby with them and made it difficult to get things done. Some of us thought he was having some sort of crisis. He hardly wanted to talk about what you might call sacramental or pastoral issues. It was all food and wine with him. We'd only ever had Irish priests in the parish before. They'd come in to take confessions.

Mrs Fraser And was that his worst crime in your view? Not bothering with Catholic care?

Mr Dorran Not really. That was just the icing. It was more noticeable the way he has with some of the pupils. My colleagues and I were aware of the fact that he saw some of them outside school hours. He seemed to cultivate the company of certain youngsters. They had a language. He took them on trips.

Mrs Fraser What sort of trips?

Mr Dorran To places of interest. Places that Father David decided were interesting. One time, he took them on a trip to Ailsa Craig. There was talk of drink being consumed.

Sheriff The bird sanctuary.

Mr Dorran Yes, My Lord.

Mrs Fraser Your headmaster, Mr McCallum, said in a statement to the police that he found it difficult to say no to Father David. Was that your experience also?

Mr Dorran In a Catholic school, it's always hard to say no to the chaplain. They have a kind of authority.

Mrs Fraser You say Mr Anderton had built some sort of relationship with these pupils. What sort of youngsters were these?

Mr Dorran What you might call the more difficult element. The . . . er . . . 'special needs' group.

Mrs Fraser And would you say these pupils are especially vulnerable as young individuals?

Mr Hamilton gets to his feet.

Mr Hamilton Objection.

Sheriff Please, Mr Hamilton. Do you really want to go this way? We've a lot to get through.

Mr Hamilton I have no interest in holding up proceedings, Your Lordship, but the question contains an inference that is beyond the power of this court to prove or disprove. Children's vulnerability is something we might take for granted without a special point being made of it in this case.

Sheriff Overruled. Please answer the question.

Mr Dorran Could it be repeated?

Mrs Fraser Would you say the pupils who make up the remedial classes of St Andrew could be described as being especially vulnerable?

Mr Dorran Yes, I probably would say that. More vulnerable and more tough as well.

The spotlight fades on Mr Dorran as Mrs Poole rises, with the aid of her sticks, and walks slowly forward. The spotlight again.

Sheriff Mrs Poole, thank you for coming to the court today. I gather you've not been in the best of health. May we offer you a seat?

She shakes her head.

Mrs Fraser Mrs Poole, am I right in stating that you previously worked for David Anderton in the chapel house at the Church of St John Ogilvie?

Mrs Poole Mondays and Fridays. And half a day on Sunday.

Mrs Fraser A Sunday morning, yes?

Mrs Poole That's right.

Mrs Fraser And would you be so kind, Mrs Poole, just in your own words, to tell the court what you saw when you arrived for work on Sunday 11 July.

Mrs Poole I'd like to say something first.

Mrs Fraser Please answer the question, Mrs Poole.

Mrs Poole Your Honour, I want to say something.

Sheriff We don't allow statements here, Mrs Poole.

Mrs Poole I know, but I want to say an important thing before answering the woman's question.

Sheriff Please be quick.

Mrs Poole Father David is not a bad man. I don't think he knows very much about people, and Dalgarnock was a strange place to him. He does not understand how they do things here . . .

Sheriff Mrs Poole –

Mrs Poole He knows so much about other things.

Sheriff I must ask you to stop, Mrs Poole.

Mrs Poole We didn't always agree about things. I have always liked music and we disagreed about some topics. But Father David was good to me and I know he was to those kids as well. They're no angels either.

Sheriff Mrs Poole! This is a court of law. I am sure you have very tender reminiscences of the accused, but we are here today to establish whether or not he has committed a criminal offence. Do you understand what I'm saying?

Mrs Poole Yes.

Sheriff Well, please confine yourself to answering the Procurator Fiscal's questions.

Mrs Poole I'm not an uncultivated woman, Your Honour.

Sheriff I have no doubt . . .

Mrs Poole No, sir. I was Father David's housekeeper. He paid for my work out of his own pocket. He paid for a great deal of things out of his own pocket, including the wine we would sometimes drink at lunch. He taught me something about how to choose it, how to taste it. I had been learning French for some time before I knew him, and then he helped me improve it with a little conversation.

Sheriff Mrs Poole –

Mrs Poole I will not be shushed by you or anybody else! I am a cultured person. And so is the accused. And perhaps you are too, sir. Are you familiar with the works of Robert Burns?

Sheriff Yes, I am, Mrs Poole. As a matter of fact, I'm Chairman of the North Ayrshire Association of Burns Clubs.

Mrs Poole Then you'll know very well, I'm sure, his 'Address to the Unco Guid'.

Sheriff NO, YOU DON'T.

Mrs Poole About the Rigid Righteous and the Rigid Wise. The whole world is full of them now. These people running through the streets and outside this court today haven't a line of poetry between them and yet, they would seek to destroy this man . . .

Sheriff MRS POOLE, I WILL NOT TELL YOU AGAIN.

Mrs Poole
'The cleanest corn that e'er was dight
May hae some pyles o' caff in –'

The Sheriff brings down his gavel with a crash.

There's yer Ayrshire wisdom.

Sheriff Mrs Poole, if there are any more outbursts of this sort, I will have no hesitation whatever in removing you from this courtroom. You are showing contempt for these proceedings, and I will not tolerate that. Am I making myself clear?

Mrs Poole Yes.

Sheriff Now, confine your remarks to what might be said in response to the questions put to you by this learned lady. Mrs Fraser.

Mrs Fraser We hear you speak in broad defence of your employer, Mrs Poole. But let us leap back. In a statement you gave to the police on the fifth of August this year you said, and I quote: 'I don't think he took his vocation very seriously. I think it's all sentiment with Father David. He lives in the past or some other place. He was stupid to take up with those menaces and I told him as much.' Are those your words, Mrs Poole?

Mrs Poole I was upset at the time.

Mrs Fraser Are these your words? Or are you now withdrawing these statements you made to the police?

Mrs Poole I am not withdrawing anything. I was upset when I made these remarks. I have not been well.

Mrs Fraser So they reflect your views at the time?

Mrs Poole Things are complicated sometimes.

Mrs Fraser Complicated you say, Mrs Poole. And was there anything complicated about what you saw when you came to start work early on the morning of 11 July?

Mrs Poole I don't understand the question.

Mrs Fraser Let me refresh your memory. In your statement, you said that David Anderton was 'stretched out in the living room surrounded by bottles of wine'.

You said he was holding Mark McNulty's hand when you entered, the young man looked inebriated, and there was a smell of hashish or 'something of that kind'. You added: 'Father David was stupid. He was hanging over that boy McNulty like a cheap suit.' Did you say these things, Mrs Poole?

Mrs Poole Yes.

Mrs Fraser And did the young man look comfortable?

Mrs Poole That young man always looks comfortable. It isn't in his nature not to be comfortable. He does what he pleases.

Mrs Fraser I put it to you that you are in no position to judge that. Mark McNulty was fifteen years old at the time of the incident. You are in no position to judge what trauma he might have suffered at the hands of David Anderton. Or what situation of trust may have been exploited.

Mrs Poole I suppose not.

Mrs Fraser One last question. You recently underwent a series of operations at Crosshouse Hospital? Is that right?

Mrs Poole Yes.

Mrs Fraser And you were under the care of the private medical wing of the hospital, I understand.

Mrs Poole does not reply.

It would appear to be the case. May I ask who paid for that private treatment, Mrs Poole?

Mr Hamilton Objection.

Sheriff Overruled.

Mrs Poole stares at Father David.

Mrs Fraser It was Mrs Anderton, the mother of the accused, was it not?

Mrs Poole continues to stare.

Mrs Poole (*to Father David*) I'm sorry.

Mrs Fraser Thank you, Mrs Poole. That will do for now.

Father David Never mind. It's all right.

The spotlight fades. Mrs Poole has gone.
   The video link comes on. Much crackling and interference.
   After some confusion, Lisa appears on screen.
   Mr Hamilton rises.

Mr Hamilton Miss Nolan, can you hear me?

Lisa Yeah. Just about.

Mr Hamilton In the year prior to meeting Father David, would you say you were a good pupil?

Lisa No' bad.

Mr Hamilton Not bad. Yet not very good, either. It appears you had a truancy problem. It also appears you had been excluded from St Andrew's on two separate occasions for unacceptable behaviour. I put it to you,

Miss Nolan, that you were the very opposite of a good pupil, and that far from Father David exploiting you and your friend, Father David was in fact very kind to you both. He took trouble with you that few other individuals would have taken, and you rewarded him by drawing him into circumstances you knew would be difficult for him. Is that not right?

Lisa Naw, it was him that wanted to go places. It was him that rang or texted us and wanted to go out. He never acted like a priest. He acted like he wanted to be our pal or something.

Mr Hamilton Mark McNulty was your boyfriend, was he not? And you were having some difficulty with one another, were you not? And you in fact became jealous of the help that Father David was giving Mark and of the innocent friendship that had grown up between them?

Lisa That's rubbish. You're twistin' everythin'. Father David couldnae take his eyes off Mark. They were glued tae 'im the whole time. He pure fancied him. Everybody knew that.

Mr Hamilton Did they, Miss Nolan? The record suggests that you could not maintain a relationship with any of your teachers. Your father was often unhappy with you. There is a suggestion here that you have been involved in several bouts of under-age drinking.

But now, Miss Nolan, we are to accept you as an excellent judge of character.

Lisa You don't know me. You don't know Mark. And you don't know him.

Mr Hamilton Oh, but you do, Miss Nolan? You know him very well? This man who has been a devoted parish priest for nearly thirty years. This man who played a part in people's lives long before you were born. This civilised man whose reputation you now play with – you know him, do you?

Lisa I know he was wrong. He didnae behave right.

Mr Hamilton Thank you for your lessons in good behaviour, Miss Nolan. We shall be sure to bear them in mind. No more questions.

Slight pause.

Lisa Is that it?

Someone in the video room indicates to her to leave the chair, which reluctantly she does. The video chair is empty as Father David turns to Mr Hamilton.

Father David I'd really prefer it if you didn't berate them. Just let their evidence speak for itself. Otherwise, it's just an unseemly scrap between my world and theirs.

Mr Hamilton Father David, I'm afraid you're out of touch with legal reality.

Father David I want you to let me take the stand.

Mr Hamilton That would be a sure recipe for disaster. You would most certainly lose.
Think of your mother.

Mark appears on the screen.

Mr McNulty. You are hearing me distinctly?

Mark Aye.

Mr Hamilton Mr McNulty, would you say you led Father David on?

Mark I wasn't in the best nick at the time.

Sheriff You *what*?

Mark I'm sorry. I wasn't in the best of health at the time.

I was drinking and . . . it was drugs. He took them with me.

Mr Hamilton Right. But, in your mind, there is no sense in which you took advantage of his generosity? You didn't abuse his weakness? It didn't occur to you that the accused might be lonely?

Mark Aye. I felt sorry for him.

Mr Hamilton And you took him to one of your drinking dens, did you, because you felt sorry for him? You danced in his sitting room for the same reason? And you lay down on the rug with him because you felt sorry for him? Is that what you would like the court to believe, Mr McNulty?

Mark He was my pal.

Mr Hamilton And you were excited to have a friend like that, were you not? A priest with a powerful position in the parish?

Mark It was just somewhere to go. He could have said no. He could have told me to go away. He was the adult, wasn't he?

Father David Please stop.

Sheriff What is it now?

Father David Will you just stop. It was my fault.

Sheriff Please sit down.

Mr Hamilton You mustn't lose your footing. We are in a stronger position than you think.

Father David You might be. I'm not. It was my fault. Never mind about the words.

Sheriff Do you wish to speak to your counsel in private?

Father David I would like to take the stand, My Lord.

A deep sigh from the Sheriff.

Sheriff Mr Hamilton?

Mr Hamilton As it is my client's wish, My Lord . . .

Father David looks at a bewildered, unseeing Mark on the screen. He turns into the spotlight.

Father David, could this situation with the young people in Dalgarnock be described as some sort of culture clash?

Father David Not really. Not in the terms you mean. When it comes down to it, I am more childish than they are. And, in relation to the things that matter to them, the young people were more pious than me.

Mr Hamilton I see.

A pause.

No more questions.

Mark's image disappears.

Sheriff David Anderton. Are you showing contempt for this court?

Father David No, Your Lordship. Not for the court. For me inside it.

Sheriff Well, I'll take that on trust. This has been a most vexing occasion. If I suspect you have been wasting my time, I will come down very hard. Do you understand?

Father David Yes, sir.

Sheriff You came to this place and pled not guilty to a charge of assaulting this young man, Mark McNulty. Do you now wish to change your plea?

Father David I hated the wording of the charge. I cannot conceive of myself as having assaulted or attacked him.

Sheriff What precisely did you do?

Father David I kissed him.

Sheriff Well, Mr Anderton. He was a fifteen-year-old boy. I'm not at all sure what country you come from, but under the laws of Scotland, in the alleged circumstances, we may call that assault.

Father David My crime, Your Lordship, if I may say so, was a crime of misrecognition. For a short time, I allowed myself to be in thrall to an unsuitable person. But I did not assault him and could not go along with myself if I perceived that I did.

Sheriff Then perhaps you might have to alter your perception, Mr Anderton. I am bound to tell you, sir, that your attitude to this court is annoying. Your remarks are obtuse. From your behaviour, sir, I dare say you imagine your case is soon to be taken down in the book of martyrs. Please allow me to tell you that it will not. You stand accused of assaulting a young man; a young man, over whom you had influence and authority. Do you understand?

Father David All too well, Your Lordship.

Sheriff You might have destroyed that young man's innocence.

Father David I rather doubt it. The young man has no innocence. I say that not in my own defence, but in his.

Sheriff That is a horrible thing to say. And to hear it from a member of Catholic clergy is shocking.

Father David I don't mean to shock anyone, only to give a precise account of the circumstances.

Sheriff We will stick to the facts.

The Procurator Fiscal rises.

Mrs Fraser Mr Anderton, after carousing on the estate with him, did you then invite this young man to your house?

Father David Yes.

Mrs Fraser At what time?

Father David It was rather late.

Mrs Fraser In the middle of the night?

Father David Yes, I'd say so.

Mrs Fraser And you plied him with drink?

Father David I opened some wine.

Mrs Fraser And you drank alongside him?

Father David I did.

Mrs Fraser And you took drugs together?

Father David Yes.

Mrs Fraser A quantity of Ecstasy tablets, we gather?

Father David Yes.

Mrs Fraser And you lay down with him on the rug?

Father David I did.

Mrs Fraser And you tried to kiss him?

Father David Yes.

Mrs Fraser And he refused?

Father David That's right.

Mrs Fraser And let me ask you one more question, Mr Anderton. If the young man had not refused, would you have gone further?

Father David Yes.

Gasps and sighs are brought to a halt by the Sheriff.

Sheriff This man, for whatever reason, fooled a community into trusting him.

He fooled them with his talk, and with his faith.

He fooled them with his background and the height of his ideals.

We are not here to try his faith. Yet the prosecution may have proved, as he himself may have proved by his own words, that his journey towards this young person was a journey of self-interest.

The law in this case does not allow for equivocation when it comes to the naming of crimes; if he did what he says he did, he has sexually assaulted this young man, and you are obliged to find him guilty.

The Sheriff's microphone clicks off abruptly, as the spotlight snaps out on Father David.

The court dissolves amid cries of 'No Pope of Rome' etc.

A mist has come down. There is a wind. Sounds of traffic.

Men and women making their way home, to pubs etc.

Father David, in a dark winter coat, is walking arm in arm with his mother.

Mrs Anderton I hoped you wouldn't mind a surprise visitor. I wasn't sure of the times.

Father David Well, I don't work in the evenings. In fact, you've coincided with my day off.

Mrs Anderton Good heavens. Days off. Nights free. What kind of penance is this? Your gaoler must be very understanding. I'm sorry not to have met him.

Father David 'Supervisor', Mother. And she's a woman.
    I'm the only part-timer. The 'inmates' are all handicapped pensioners. Many of them have never left Ayrshire. They've stayed on the farm, cleaning tools and haunting the greenhouses. Their years have passed in the company of rabbits and annual shows of strawberries.

Mrs Anderton And how much longer are you bound to serve this community?

Father David The Sheriff gave me a hundred days and I've been toiling for two months.

Mrs Anderton You'll be freed in time for Christmas.

They are now on their own.

And then?

Father David Then perhaps fortune might turn once more in my favour and allow me to go from Scotland in a state of peace – with a heart reconciled to the terms of my disgrace.

Mrs Anderton What a marvellous sentence!
    The words, I mean.

Father David laughs.

Perhaps one day you'll write something.

Father David Could you brook a rival?

Mrs Anderton My books have worked well enough, but I think you could do better.

Something more searching. I'm afraid I don't have much of what your old friend Proust called 'ascending power'.

Father David You give yourself too little credit, Mother. I've probably used up all my circumspection on old hymns and riotous living.

Mrs Anderton Doesn't sound like it.

Ever since you were young, you've looked at things with feeling.

You see the shape of things.

When you opted to become a priest, I remember thinking it was that quality that might serve you well. But we were talking about writing. It's customary for writers to be made by their parents. With us, it was the other way round.

I'm sure I became a novelist to keep up with you.

Father David Not true. It's your own gift.

Mrs Anderton I'm rather proud of the fact. My outer child gave my inner child a job.

Father David You're mad.

Mrs Anderton I'm too old and too grand to care.
And I must get back.

Father David Why? You've only just got here.

Mrs Anderton Oh, the Muse, you know . . . and the trains are so erratic.

Father David But you drove down.

Mrs Anderton It's time you had your own car again.

She hands him the keys.

Father David Mother . . .

Mrs Anderton Now, don't make me use up any old clichés. I need them all for my books.

He kisses her cheek.

I might just risk an aphorism.

Father David What?

Mrs Anderton Always trust a stranger. It's often the people we know who let us down.
 Don't forget your way back.

Father David I won't. You're so practical, Mother.

Mrs Anderton I know. But what else is there?

She leaves Father David looking at his new keys.

A flickering light in the mist.
 A new red bicycle crosses the stage on one wheel.

Father David Mark?

The bicycle returns.
 On hearing his name, Mrs Anderton lingers for a few moments in the mist and watches, unseen by either of them.

Mark Hiya, Father!

Father David Mark. How are you?

Mark keeps cycling round energetically, like a circus performer.

Mark Not bad. What you up to?

Father David Peeling carrots.

Mark Wicked.

Father David Apparently.

Mark laughs.

New bike?

Mark Borrowed it.

Father David Oh yes?

Mark Gotta keep fit.
I've left school.

Father David Why so soon?
You're clever, Mark. Too clever to give up on your education so early.

Mark I'm going into the army. Next week it is. I'm going to Plymouth for training.
They give you a trade and everything.

Father David Yes.

Mark The army needs people. You know that. There's a war on. They say it's finished but nobody believes that.

Father David I doubt it'll be finished for a long time.

Mark Good. Plenty of work, then. They might even send me out to where it's all happening.

Father David You wouldn't want that.

Mark Why not? We're making a difference out there. You told me yourself it's the right thing.

Mrs Anderton has slipped away, unnoticed.

You've got to have your team, Father.

Father David Yes, you told me that before.

Mark Have you ever known any soldiers?

Father David No, but I knew their names. They were carved into a wall at the old college I went to.

Mark So you didn't know any then?

Father David What about your Irish Republican Army? I don't suppose they'd be very pleased with your choice of career.

Mark My dad says that's all over for now. And it's not as if they're going to give me a trade, is it?

He cycles round.

Lisa's pregnant.

Father David Oh dear.

Mark Don't be like that. She's happy enough.

Father David Is the baby yours?

Mark Nope. Nuttin' to do with me.

Father David God bless her.

Mark Ah, save it. Lisa's cool. She's keeping it. She'll be good at being somebody's maw.

Father David She's so young.

Mark stops cycling.

Mark It wasn't all bad, Father, was it? We had a few laughs.

Mark extends his hand.

Father David Wherever you go, Mark, look after yourself.

They shake hands. Mark cycles off.

Mark Look out for me on the telly!

It has started to snow.
  Father David finds himself recalling some lines of William Cowper.

Father David

'I sometimes think myself inclined
To love Thee, if I could;
But often feel another mind,
Averse to all that's good.'

His phone rings. He sees the name.

Mrs Poole! Or may I call you Anne? Oh, Mr Poole . . .
I thought it was . . .

A pause.

Oh, I see . . . I'm so sorry. I am so, so sorry.
Yes . . . yes . . .
Well, perhaps I could take . . . No . . . no.
No, of course, I understand.
Um . . . Bach, I think.

A Bach Cantata.
*A small Christmas tree on a small table. It flashes on
and off.*
Two glasses. Two chairs. A newspaper.
Jack Poole is opening a bottle of white wine.

SCENE SEVEN

Mr Poole You're a good time-keeper.

*Father David brushes the snow from his hair and takes
off his coat.*

Father David Oh, yes. I set off early to enjoy the weather.

Mr Poole It would put years on you, so it would.

Father David I hope that's not too cold for you.

Mr Poole I don't usually drink white. But I'm drinking
this one. This'll be the good stuff, eh?

Father David Not bad. Just right for today.

He lifts the newspaper to sit down.

You like reading the newspaper?

Mr Poole Once you get past the rubbish.

Father David My father said you couldn't call yourself a man until you could read the local paper from cover to cover and find every item interesting.

Mr Poole The sport's good. I like to see how the teams are doing.

Mr Poole fills their glasses.

What did he do, your father?

Father David He was a surgeon. I didn't really know him. He died of a coronary when I was quite young. My mother used to say he was good at mending other people's hearts, but he couldn't mend his own.

Mr Poole I've been reading about them celebrating in Iraq.

Father David Celebrating?

Mr Poole Christmas.

Father David Of course.

They clink glasses and drink.

Mr Poole Pure magic.

Father David Yes.

Mr Poole Now, that's what I call a glass of wine.

They drink in silence.

It's all religion, isn't it?

He reaches over and switches the tree light to its constant mode.

Not that I've anything against religion. But those young fellas could be out there for years.

Father David I hope not.

Mr Poole Anne used to say that half of them don't have a clue why they're out there.

Father David No. Maybe those boys should be at home with their families.

Mr Poole It's all just fear, isn't it? We're frightened of them, and they're frightened of us, and it's all just a mess.

He fills their glasses.

Father David This is tremendously good, isn't it?

Mr Poole Anne would have certainly have appreciated it.

Father David Yes. She would.

Mr Poole puts down his glass.

Mr Poole I wish I could have some of the years back, so we could have given it another try.

Father David We all want that. I believe we want it from the moment we know how to want things.

Mr Poole My mother died of cancer.

Father David I know. Mrs Poole mentioned it once.

Mr Poole tops them up.

Mr Poole It's back to the single life. Or maybe I've always been living the single life. Maybe everybody does. You have.

Father David I thought I was supposed to be king of the double life.

Mr Poole That's only them talking.

He indicates the newspaper.

It'll be just me here now. That's the hardest part.

Father David It will just take time.

Mr Poole That's right.

He raises his glass.

Merry Christmas.

Father David And to you.

Mr Poole Where will you go now?

Father David Oh, there are places I've been happy. It may be time to find them again.

Mr Poole That's good.

Father David I've been a very mediocre caretaker of my own faith.

Mr Poole Will you not stay for a bite to eat?

Father David Thank you, no. I'm on the move.

They drink in silence.

Mr Poole Well. This hasn't been a bad wee drink at all.

Father David Perfect. *Parfait.*

Father David pulls on his coat.

Goodbye, Mr Poole.

Mr Poole Jack.

Father David Jack.

Mr Poole Goodbye, Father.

They shake hands.

David.

He buttons his coat. Mr Poole drinks the last of the wine.

A blustery wind as table, chairs and Mr Poole disappear.

David takes his car keys from his coat pocket.

He takes in a satisfying gulp of air and finds himself recalling some lines of Tennyson.

David

'Be near me when I fade away,
To point the term of human strife,
And on the low dark verge of life
The twilight of eternal day.'

He throws his keys up and catches them as he walks towards an iridescent yellow sky.

Birdsong. A silhouette.